XmAS 2002

Anne,
Love From 'Mary

THIS IS
NOT A
NOVEL

BY JENNIFER JOHNSTON

The Captains and the Kings*
The Gates*
How Many Miles to Babylon?
Shadows on our Skin*
The Old Jest
The Christmas Tree*
The Railway Station Man*
Fool's Sanctuary*
The Invisible Worm*
The Illusionist
Two Moons*
The Gingerbread Woman*

(*Also available in Review)

THIS IS

NOT A

NOVEL

JENNIFER JOHNSTON

review

First published in 2002 by REVIEW

An imprint of Headline Book Publishing

10 9 8 7 6 5 4 3 2 1

Cataloguing in Publication Data is available from the British Library

ISBN 0 7472 6945 9

Printed and bound in Great Britain by Clays Ltd, St Ives plc

Typeset in Centaur by Avon Data Ltd, Bidford-on-Avon, Warwickshire

Designed by Peter Ward Design

HEADLINE BOOK PUBLISHING
A division of Hodder Headline
338 Euston Road, London NW1 3BH

www.reviewbooks.co.uk
www.hodderheadline.com

For Lelia,
A woman of many arts and parts
And a great friend,
With love.

This is not a novel.

I want to make that perfectly clear.

Normally when I set out to write a piece of fiction, I invent a setting, a landscape, a climate, a world, in fact, that has no reality outside the pages of the book, and into that world I insert my characters. I become the puppet master and I tweak and push these wretches, who, like us, have never asked to be born, through all sorts of contortions, until that merciful moment when I type those exultant words 'The End'.

A bit like God, really, who I'm sure had the best intentions when he created the world and then popped those two innocents into his Garden of Eden. Did he, at that moment, sit back, fold his hands and smile at his own handiwork? If so he must have got the shock of his life when that old serpent slithered on to the scene and blew his scenario sky high.

I am not sure into what category this piece of writing should fall.

I would like to think that rather than a scrappy memoir it might be a *cri de coeur*, a hopeful message sent out into the world, like a piece of paper in a bottle dropped into the sea; my hope being that my brother Johnny, somewhere in the world, I believe, may read it and may pick up the nearest telephone.

Having said that, may I return to the beginning?

The title.

The notion of this piece of writing had been in my mind for some time and was rather energetically seeking a way to get out, like a bird shut in a room, fluttering, flapping and shitting from time to time on the carpet. Then one day I wandered, somewhat aimlessly, into an exhibition of the work of René Magritte, a painter whose work, until then, I had seen mainly in reproduction. Postcard-sized jokes they'd always seemed to me and suddenly here I was being surprised and moved by the meticulous lunacy with which the artist viewed the world; in particular the bourgeois world, from which, I reluctantly have to admit, I come. These were far from light-hearted jokes: they were more like government health warnings, enjoy if you insist, but beware. Nothing here is what it seems to be.

Ceci n'est pas une pomme!

For several weeks I kept seeing in my mind's eye that apple on its little twig with the green leaf attached: as real, it seemed to me, and as tempting, as the apple in the Garden of Eden.

What would have happened, I wondered, if that serpent, at the last moment, just as Eve was about to take that fateful bite, had said softly into her ear, 'And by the way, Madame, *ceci n'est pas une pomme*'?

Would she have clobbered him with a fig leaf and thrown the apple away? In which case, would the world now be a very different place, filled with harmony and love, fraternal feelings everywhere, nobody eating apples or writing books more subversive than 'Noddy in Toyland'?

I have always amused myself with such fooleries: they inject little spurts of energy into the bloodstream; they are small mental fixes.

Anyway, having seen that picture and let the thought of it sit for a while in my mind I came to the conclusion that I should send my brother a message, and this seems to be the only way in which I may be able to manage to do it. He may not, of course, be interested in my conclusions, nor may he believe them; that is his privilege. At least I will have tried to let him know how much I love him and how for years I have longed to see him home again. At least, that is the message I intend to send, but who knows? Once the screen is up and the words start to patter out from under the fingers, nothing ever happens as you have planned it. Like in the Garden of Eden, the serpent may slither in and put paid to all my well-laid plans.

* * *

I have just sold my father's house in Lansdowne Road for a whacking amount of money. With the help of my solicitor, Mr Downey, Johnny's share has been put aside for him safely and, I hope, judiciously. Mr Downey thinks I am quite foolish to do this. He is convinced, as were both my parents, that Johnny is dead; that Johnny drowned on 17 September 1970. Nearly thirty years ago.

❊ ❊ ❊

I was eighteen years two months and two days when my father came to see me in the nursing home and told me that Johnny was dead.

Drowned.

Lost at sea.

Johnny was two years seven months and three days older than I was, making him on that day round about twenty years and nine months, give or take a day or two. I had asked for a calendar on the day that I had started to speak again, and it hung by the window; when the wind blew, the pages would flicker and rustle together, as if for a few moments they were alive. I cancelled each day that passed with a neat black stroke, an acute accent, driving upwards from left to right. Seven strokes and then another seven and so on, until the evening came when I would turn the page and a whole new month would stretch ahead of me, the days undefiled.

The day my father came to tell me the news I had been over six months in the home. For the first month I had not spoken a word or laughed or even cried aloud. From time to time silent tears would wet my cheeks.

It was a beautiful sunny autumn evening and I was walking in the garden. It was charming, with neat beds and grassy walks through the trees. The leaves were turning from the tired green of late summer to gold and brown and orange. A few other patients, all much older than I, walked beneath the trees or sat in the benign evening sun and breathed the still warm air. I could hear their feet brushing from time to time through the leaves that had been blown early from the trees. There were a few roses remaining in the bed at the bottom of the garden and I was staring at the soft, crumpled petals when my nurse spoke just behind me. I was startled by her voice. I had, in my mind, been a long way away.

'Imogen,' she said. 'Your father . . .'

I turned. She was dressed in blue that day, and my father stood behind her, pale and fretful-looking.

'. . . is here to . . .'

He smiled a rapid smile in my direction and nodded his head.

'. . . see you. Imogen . . .'

'Yes,' I said. 'Hello, Father.'

He nodded again in my direction. He looked awful,

more than just fretful. He looked shattered. Maybe, I thought, with malice and probably a little madness – that, after all, was why I was there – Sylvia has self-destructed.

Sylvia was my mother.

'I will leave you together, Doctor.' The nurse was speaking to him. 'I will be above on the terrace if you feel you need me.'

She patted me on the shoulder, turned and walked away across the grass, her blue dress flipping from side to side as she moved. She wore white shoes, like nurses did in American films; a sartorial mistake, I have always thought.

My father came towards me. He put an arm around my shoulders and kissed the air beside my right cheek. 'Imogen.'

I said nothing. I had become very good at saying nothing.

'Let's sit down. Or are you cold?'

I shook my head.

He nodded towards an empty wooden seat and we walked across the grass, his arm still protectively and paternally across my shoulders.

When we had sat down he took a handkerchief from his pocket and dabbed at his forehead, then he cleared his throat.

'How's Sylvia?' I asked politely.

He took my hand. 'Your mother's fine . . . well . . . fine . . . under the . . . yes . . . under the . . . Your mother's . . .' His voice trailed away, blown on a little autumnal gust of wind. 'No. It's . . . Johnny.'

'Johnny?'

'Yes. I . . . we . . . didn't know whether . . . whether.'

'If there's something to tell, please, Father, tell me.' I dug my nails into his hand.

Johnny.

'He's dead.'

There was a very long silence. Somewhere across the grass a woman laughed. A loud and rather raucous laugh. I can hear it now, echoing down the years.

'Drowned.'

He almost whispered the word. I didn't believe that I had heard it right.

'He . . . ?'

'Drowned.'

'No.' I laughed. 'You're joking. No.'

He was hurting my hand now, so tight he was holding it. 'It is as I say, Imogen. Ten days ago. The seventeenth of this month.'

'How could Johnny drown?'

'I didn't want to tell you, but your mother and Dr Craig insisted. I thought wait. Let us wait until she is stronger, more able to —'

'How could Johnny drown?'

'– cope.'

'Answer me, Father. How?'

'The . . . the Gardai say that is what must have happened. Your mother saw him swimming out, round the point. She described it over and over again. Out. The sun shone on his flashing arms . . . That was how she put it. She thought nothing of it. There were black stormclouds way out to sea, but she thought nothing of that either. She—'

'It doesn't matter what she saw. Johnny couldn't drown.'

'That's what I would have thought too, but I'm afraid, Imogen, that the truth has to be faced.'

'Was he . . . was he . . . did they find a . . . ?'

He let go of my hand and rubbed at his face. 'No. Not yet. No . . . But, Imogen, the Gardai . . .'

'I don't care about the Gardai. He couldn't drown. I know that. The police don't realise . . .'

'Your mother . . .'

'I don't care what Mother saw. She should know as well as I do that Johnny—'

'He swam out to sea and he never came back.'

I couldn't bear the conversation for another moment. I stood up. 'I think I would like to go inside now.' I turned away from him and walked across the shaved grass to the terrace, where the windows were still open to let the last of the sun in to warm the rooms and where the nurse in the blue dress was waiting for me.

'Imogen,' he called after me, and I paid no heed.

'Imogen.'

When I reached my room on the first floor, I took a pen from the table by my bed and, pressing hard on the ball point, I blackened out the date: 27 September, a beautiful autumn day, no longer existed.

✻ ✻ ✻

As well as the house in Lansdowne Road we had a house in County Cork called Paradise.

It was an old stone house built about two hundred years ago that had been bought by my great-grandfather at the beginning of the twentieth century. It sat on the side of a hill overlooking a bay, with fields stretching below it down to the sea. A path through a little grove of trees led to a boathouse and a small jetty. It was from this jetty that Johnny was supposed to have swum out to sea.

We used to spend all our holidays in Paradise, as had my father and his father before him. I had always presumed that one day it would belong to Johnny and me, but not long after Johnny's disappearance my father sold the house and it is now a modest country-house hotel, and a haven, or so it says in the brochures, for lovers of water sports.

They have changed the name of the house to Bealtaine, which means May in the Irish language. Don't ask me why they did this, I presume they felt that to call a hotel Paradise was asking for trouble. The word Bealtaine has a charm to it, even if you don't know what it means.

I live now in a neat house in Sandycove, in a road tipping down to the sea. I have to live near the sea; I don't want to be in it or on it, but I find it hard to live without the sound of it, the smell of it and the constant reflection of the sky, clouds, night, day, grey, blue, and I love the turbulence of storms.

My house is painted yellow, easy for taxi drivers: 'The yellow house, third gate up on the right.' The front garden is full of rose bushes. It was like that when I bought the house and I saw no reason to change it.

I took little from my father's house after he died, some books, the piano, which I play without much talent but it was my great-grandmother's Broadwood small grand, and nothing on earth would have persuaded me to sell it. I am lucky to have the room to house it. Also, and really the most important thing, was a large trunk full of papers, letters, diaries, press cuttings and old photographs, all pertaining to his family.

Sylvia was not a magpie like my father was. Her study was almost bare: only medical textbooks on the shelves, and on her desk neatly stacked medical journals and well-filed case notes. Nothing personal at all. No pictures of her parents or siblings, or of Johnny and myself as charming, smiling babies. She never kept postcards from friends on holiday or theatre programmes; no mementoes or memories hung around in her private rooms. It was as if she didn't want to know of the existence of yesterday.

* * *

Having blackened out 27 September on the calendar, I went and sat on my bed and waited for the nurse to come.

Johnny floated into my head, a trail of ruffled water behind him, his eyes shut against the sun. I sat on a rock and watched him, my feet dangling into the sea. As he floated past me he spoke. 'Hey ho, Imogen.'

'Hey ho, Johnny.'

'*Is' gut, ja?*'

'*Is' gut,* Johnny.'

I leaned down and scooped a handful of water and threw the glittering drops towards his body. He opened his eyes and turned over on to his stomach.

'*Meine Schwester ist ein Schweinchen.*'

He began to swim, with his strong crawl, out to sea, his head rolling sideways and down, sideways and down, his arms dazzling with drops as he swam directly along the path of the sun. My eyes hurt as I watched him.

'Johnny,' I called.

Onny came back the echo from the cliffs that sheltered the west side of the bay.

On . . . ny.

'Johnny.'

O . . . oo . . . onny.

'Come back.'

Ack.

Aaa . . . ck.

Always the second echo was fractured, as if the word hitting the rocks had been broken into fragments.

Slowly he turned and swam back towards me. He climbed up the ladder on to the jetty and walked out on to the diving board. He clicked his fingers in my direction to make sure he had my attention and then dived, his body spinning and turning over and over before he sliced, hardly ruffling the water, into the sea.

'Bravo. Oh, bravo, Johnny.'

He leaped up through the water, one hand in the air waving triumphantly, then he swam towards me.

'Does that have a name? It's wonderful. I didn't know you could do that. You make it look so easy.'

He climbed on to the rock where I was sitting. Water ran from his hair; he shone in the sun.

'Sometimes it works and sometimes it doesn't.'

'Who taught you? Daddy couldn't have taught you that.'

Johnny laughed. 'Not Daddy. He's a coward when it comes to diving. I worked that out ages ago. Have you noticed the way he tenses up the moment he starts to prepare a dive? Every bit of him gets rigid. No one can do a good dive like that.'

'Who, then?'

'One of the masters at school. He's a genius. It's like watching a bird flying when you watch him dive.'

'Does he have a name? Have I heard you speak about him before?'

'Bruno Schlegel. He's a student teacher, really. Just here for a year or two.'

'Teaching you all diving?'

'No, stupid. German. The diving is a bonus.' He stood up and held out his hand to me. 'Come on. I'll give you five and race you to the rock.' He pulled me to my feet. 'Starting now.' He began to count. 'One, two, three . . .'

When it came to swimming, Johnny always used to win.

* * *

I sat on the bed.

The cover was pink and floral, matching the curtains, which trembled slightly in the breeze.

I kept my windows open when they would allow me.

There were bars on the outside of the windows.

Painted white.

I think they thought that made it all right.

White bars.

Johnny had never come to visit me in all the time that I had been there. Maybe I am wrong about that, maybe he had come in those weeks before I began to speak again. I have little recollection of that time: I only know that they filled me full of drugs and I moved in a haze of unknowing. They were trying to make me find my voice and at the same time lose the memory of what that voice wanted to say.

They were very kind. I do have to say that.

I was only a child, after all; a misguided, moderately demented child.

But that day, 27 September the day that I had blackened out on the calendar, I was eighteen years two months and two days. I was no longer a child.

They must all have been aware of that.

I became aware that the nurse had come in.

She crossed the room in her white shoes and closed down both windows. The calendar pages stopped rustling. She came over and stood beside me. I stared at the white shoes, slightly apart on the dusky pink carpet. All colour-coded the rooms, in calm pastel colours, guaranteed to soothe fevered brains.

'I've just come to see how you are,' said the nurse.

'Thank you.'

'Would you like me to get you a cup of tea?'

'Father said . . .'

'It's all right, Imogen. Matron told me. I'm so sorry.'

'It's not true.'

'Your father . . .'

'My father doesn't always tell the truth . . . Sometimes he doesn't bother to find out the truth. He can be quite a lazy man.'

I looked up and smiled into her blue eyes; they matched her dress.

'He's just gone away. He always said he would go away. He's flown . . . swum, I should say. He's not dead.'

'Your father's a doctor, dear. I think he should know what he's talking about.' She was filling a glass with water.

'Doctor schmocter.'

The nurse came towards me with the glass of water in one hand and a bottle of pills in the other. 'Matron said to give you one of these.'

I said nothing. I just stared at the blueness of her. I thought . . . Oh, shit, not again.

'Imogen . . .'

'I don't need pills. I can manage without pills. I've had enough pills since I came in here to—'

'To lessen the pain. To make you sleep and then . . .'

'No, thank you.'

The nurse looked uneasy. 'Matron . . .'

'If my brother were dead I would want to feel pain. I would want to lie awake all night and think about him and grieve for him. I would want to scream and cry if I felt like it. Disturb the other patients if need be. Matron doesn't like that. I've noticed that Matron likes silence and calm.'

She had shaken a pill from the bottle and held it out towards me. 'It's for your own good. We don't want you to harm yourself in any way.'

I laughed. 'I have never, never had any intention of harming myself.'

'Just one, Imogen. Hold out your hand, please. Otherwise . . .'

I held out my hand and she laid the pill on my palm. It looked like a shiny black insect. 'I hate it when you say otherwise,' I said.

I put the pill in my mouth and wondered whether to hide it in the space under my tongue or swallow it.

The nurse put the glass into my hand.

I decided to hide it.

'I know what you're up to,' said the nurse. 'I'm not as green as I'm cabbage-looking. Just swallow it down, there's a good girl, and don't let's have any trouble.'

I knew when I was beaten. I took the glass from her and

swallowed the pill. Life is much easier in a place like that if you practise obedience. I had learned that much.

The nurse pulled back the bedcover and pushed me gently down among the pillows. 'You'll feel better when you've had a little sleep. I'll pull the curtains over.'

'No. No, please, don't do that. I hate the curtains pulled. I hate the dark.'

'No problem. If you need me just give the bell a tinkle.' She pulled the door closed behind her.

I listened to her shoes squeaking along the passage and then there was silence and the sun went behind a cloud; the light in the room became dim. I wanted to raise my head, stretch out a hand and find my book, but a heavy hand lay on my forehead, pressing my head down into the pillows.

Whose hand?

I remember thinking that. Whose hand?

Johnny's arms drove through the water.

'Imogen,' he called.

Ogen.

Ooo . . . ennn.

* * *

I found some diaries written by my father in the trunk, the scribbled pages interleaved with cuttings and letters. The black leather books bulged and were held closed by wide elastic bands, some of them now perished.

The trunk had been locked with a padlock. I had no idea where the key might be so I telephoned a friend who had a box of efficient, well-cared-for tools and he came round and sawed the lock off for me.

'Maybe there's a body in there,' he said cheerfully to me, as he left the house.

The trunk sat silently in my workroom for about ten days before I took my courage in both hands and opened it. A slight smell of must rose with the lid, nothing more threatening.

Father had been a spasmodic diarist and I, to begin with, a spasmodic reader, but it was after I had foraged through the whole pile of stuff and looked through all the old albums, at people whose faces had familiar features but whose names I could only guess at, that the notion of writing this public appeal to Johnny came into my mind. Washing dirty linen in public, some people might call it, but I don't care. Maybe it will serve its purpose.

IRISH TIMES
8 July 1955.
Bailey. To Dr Edward and Dr Sylvia Bailey, née Tooley, a daughter, Imogen. Many thanks to the staff at the Rotunda Hospital.

A slightly tattered and discoloured piece of paper, stuck to the head of the page. Underneath is written his comment on my arrival.

Six Ibs and seven oz. As far as one can see, all faculties intact. Little hair and what there is is pale and wispy, but give her time. She looks a bit like my grandmother Bailey, strong eyebrows and a long nose. She seems hungry. A good thing. Children who are fussy eaters are so tiresome. Sylvia would have preferred another boy. She hasn't said so, but I can see it in her face and I know she finds men more congenial than women. I have no strong views. No matter what Church and Government may have to say on the subject I believe two children to be quite enough for any couple to produce. Sylvia and I have now performed one of our purposes. We have reproduced ourselves.

Not exactly welcoming, I thought, when I read his comments, but after a while, like two or three days, I had to laugh. I was glad to feel that he had commented on my likeness to his grandmother, a formidable mother of eight. I love that feeling of continuity, of having been planted somewhere in the past.

I took an old sepia picture of my great-grandmother from the bottom of the trunk, where it had lain for so many years, wrapped with care in tissue paper, and I had it framed and it hangs here now on the wall to the right of my desk. Her face is amiable, perhaps a touch arrogant, but that may be an illusion created by the length of her nose. She is sitting with her hands folded in her silk lap, surrounded by six of her eight children and with the feathery fronds of ferns filling the background space. Her eldest son, my grandfather, is not present; nor is my great-uncle Harry, who at the moment the picture was taken was about to be killed at Suvla Bay.

There is a note on the back of the picture, presumably written by my great-grandfather.

Arthur (Captain, Dublin Fusiliers) and Harry (2nd Lt the same) were serving in France and Gallipoli when this picture was taken on 15 August 1915. The news of Harry's death reached us the following week at Paradise in County Cork. Even though he is not in this picture he will be remembered for ever. God be merciful unto us and bless us and show us the light of his countenance.

There is no sign on the faces of the people in the picture of the possibility of tragedy. They merely stare at the photographer with pleasant, incurious eyes. Everyone in that picture is dead now and, indeed, most of their children, and their grandchildren are scattered around the world. I would know few of them if I were to meet them in the street.

Would I know Johnny?

I always like to think so.

In with the carefully wrapped picture of my great-grandmother was a picture of a young man in uniform. Long nose, fair hair brushed smoothly back. He holds his hat neatly under his right arm and smiles a bit forlornly at the camera. In tight black writing on the mount of the picture are the words: '1st October 1914. A present for my dear mother, all love Harry.' On the back under the name of the photographers, a firm in Grafton Street Dublin, was a verse in another hand:

> *He shall not hear the bittern cry*
> *In the wild sky, where he is lain,*
> *Nor voices of the sweeter birds*
> *Above the wailing of the rain.*

* * *

I have a picture taken of Johnny the year he won the schools' interprovincial swimming championship.

He doesn't look forlorn. Actually he is smirking.

I said that to him at the time: 'Look at that smirk on your face, gobshite.'

'I won,' was all he said back to me. 'So what's wrong with smirking?'

Put him in uniform, with his hat tucked neatly under his right arm, wipe the smirk from his face and he would be a ringer for Great-uncle Harry.

Harry.

Arry.

Arr . . . ry.

We echo and re-echo down the years.

* * *

Waking each morning is like being born.

I come out of silence and the dark and hear, softly to begin with, the stirrings of the world: first my own breathing, then gradually the normal daily sounds begin to impinge. The movement of air in the room, perhaps the drip of a tap or a gurgle somewhere in a wastepipe, a distant voice, a bird, a laugh, the sound of a car passing in the street. The light begins to prise open my protecting eyelids and, bit by bit, I start to realise that I am still alive.

I remember wondering what day it was. Had a whole

night passed since my father had come and told me in the garden that Johnny was dead?

Or a week?

Or a hundred years?

What age will I be when I open my eyes?

I remember thinking that.

I lay there realising that whatever day or year it was going to be when I opened my eyes I was going to have to work out a plan of campaign.

I must remember to believe that Johnny is dead.

I must remember to smile sadly at them when they speak to me about this, which they surely will.

I must remember not to argue; to follow where they lead. I will speak when I am spoken to; I will dance to their tune; but never again will I lose my voice.

I will . . .

At that moment the door opened and the tentative steps of the nurse moved across the room towards my bed. There was the sound of a cup being placed on the table by my bed. The sound of soft breaths.

Soft breaths.

'You're awake so?'

I opened my eyes.

Today she was dressed in green, a pale peppermint green; her apron crackled with starch.

'How did you know?'

'You had that look about you. I can tell someone awake with their eyes shut. Haven't I years of practice? Are you rested? You look rested. Didn't I say a nice sleep would do you the world of good?'

'Thank you.'

'I've left you a nice cup of tea. Take your time getting up. There's no rush.'

'What day is it? I mean, yesterday or . . . when? I don't remember. I don't know how long I've been asleep.'

'Thursday morning.' She looked down at her watch, neatly pinned to the top of her apron. 'Ten fifteen. You've slept for well over twelve hours. Isn't that good? Breakfast's over, but I could slip down and get you a bit of toast if you'd like.'

'I'm not hungry, thanks all the same.'

'A biscuit?'

I shook my head.

'Well, drink up your tea, there's a good girl, and I'll be back in a while. Perhaps you'd like a little run in the garden before lunch?'

I laughed. I wanted to bark at her, but I thought it might not be prudent.

'Perhaps,' I said.

'And Matron would like a few words with you. So the morning will be busy enough. Drink up your tea before it gets cold.'

A thought came into my mind. 'It is just tea?' I asked. 'Just . . . you know . . . tea?'

'It's just tea.'

* * *

Our mother – Sylvia, as we had been taught to call her – had soft, brown curling hair and a sweet smile; a smile like a little girl, disingenuous, innocent, showing quite a lot of white teeth. She, like my father, was a doctor, but she had given up full-time work after Johnny was born and had run three clinics a week for mothers and babies in a city-centre hospital. She would smile at the mothers and babies and they would like her before she had even spoken to them.

'We'd like to see Dr Bailey,' mothers always said, when they rang to make appointments.

Of course, it wasn't always possible: there were only so many mothers and babies you could fit in between two and five on Mondays, Wednesdays and Fridays. She didn't go in for the seamier side of family medicine at all: no child abuse, rape, wife-beating or alcohol problems came her way. She only read about them in the papers.

'Tttt,' I heard her say once. 'How can people be so awful?' She rattled the pages and turned to something less upsetting.

There is a vicious streak in me. I make no apologies for it. Perhaps it is in all of us, except possibly Father, who kept his distance from us and gave the appearance of a man absorbed totally in his work.

'We fit so well together,' Sylvia had said, one evening at dinner, 'Edward and I. He keeps the wolf from the door and I put icing on the cake.'

Johnny had laughed.

She turned towards him. 'And what is so funny?'

'Never mind. I don't suppose you've ever heard of a mixed metaphor.'

'You're so sharp,' she said, unsmiling, 'you'll cut yourself one day.'

That would have been Johnny's last year at school and, in fact, the someone to whom she spoke those words would have been Bruno Schlegel, who had come to spend the Easter holidays with us at Paradise, ostensibly to brush up Johnny's German for the Leaving Cert, but the weather had been strangely kind and the two young men had spent most of their time either in or on the water.

They never took me with them.

'Johnny. Bruno,' I would call mournfully across the bay. *Ohnny . . . uno.*

The little boat had red sails. It sliced and cavorted over the spring waves, cavorted like a red bird.

O . . . onny . . . u . . . nnoo.

It flirted with the sea and I was disconsolate; lonely, I suppose would be a better word. I was also jealous.

'I presume,' my mother said one day, as we watched the distant boat from the drawing-room window, 'that they're speaking German.'

I doubted it, but I said nothing.

One morning, though, just a couple of days before we were due to return to Dublin, I was awakened by a whistling beneath my window. I stuck my head out and saw Johnny and Bruno below me on the grass.

'*Schwester.*'

'What on earth time is it?'

Mist lay in fingers on the fields below the house and the birds still sounded sleepy.

'Irrelevant, Im. Do you want to come with us?'

'Now?'

Bruno spoke. '*Ja*, Imogen. *Komm mit.*'

I loved the way he spoke my name, drawing out the O like a long, long sigh. I blushed. I used to hate that about myself, the impossibility of controlling the heat sweeping up from my heart, it seemed, to the very top of my head.

'If your hair was longer I could climb up it,' he called. '*Komm*, Rapunzel.'

'What about breakfast?'

'For God's sake, Im, get your priorities right.'

'OK. I'll be after you in a tick.'

I remember that day still: the wind was jaunty and warm from the south, the water chuckled under the boat like a jokey friend and sent up diamond spray when we went about.

I never liked to wear shoes in the boat, but the two of them wore navy canvas shoes and white socks, which made me laugh to myself as I ran after them through the damp grass. I had never known Johnny to wear shoes in the boat before and as for socks . . . I hadn't even known he owned a pair of white socks.

Johnny gave me a push towards the stern as I jumped on board. 'It's your boat today.'

I felt the idiotic blush rising up and covering my face.

I sat down and took hold of the tiller. 'Can we go anywhere?'

'America, if you wish.'

'Dreamtime. What's got into you?'

The bay was quite small, ringed by hills; the cliffs where sea birds nested and the echo lived were on the western side of the bay's mouth where it stretched out into the sea. I decided that I would loop the bay, running close inshore to inspect the two sandy beaches and the fields that sloped right down to the edge of the water, and the village, just a few small houses and a shop clustered round the pier where I hoped that maybe some friends might be up and about so that I could wave at them as we sailed past. Then, I thought out through the mouth into the sea where the wind would be brisker and I could make the boat fly through the sea, cutting air and water, making no sound. 'I'm going to make her dance,' I called to Johnny.

'Just as long as you don't capsize her . . . or frighten Bruno.'

The German laughed. 'I don't frighten easy. I like to live life dangerously.'

'Right. Here we go, then.' I changed my plans and headed straight out towards the mouth of the bay. The sails curved and stretched, curious gulls hovered above us, and from the echo cliff I could hear the sound of hundreds of kittiwakes screeching to each other. I headed across the path of the sun towards the distant shipping lanes where I could see the slowly moving ships going about their business.

Bruno and Johnny talked softly to each other in a mixture of German and English as if I were not there. They laughed a lot and leaned towards each other, their shoulders touching from time to time, and once Bruno put out a hand and gently touched Johnny's face. I watched, and the boat ran through the water, and Johnny twitched from time to time at the sheets that held the sails, letting them out or tightening them according to the vagaries of the wind.

'Im.'

I had retreated into the silence of the wind and the chuckling of the water beneath the boat so I was startled by the sound of his voice calling to me.

'Im.'

No one else in the world has ever called me Im. I used to pretend that I hated it, despised this abbreviation of my name, but in reality I enjoyed the intimacy with him that the sound of the syllable gave me.

'Hello.'

'Why are you heading for the Bay of Biscay?'

'You said I could go wherever I wanted.'

'Open sea is so boring.'

'I'm sorry. Where would you prefer to go? America? Africa? Just say the word.'

'Perhaps a nice beach where we could drink beer and swim.'

'About.'

I pulled the tiller towards me, they ducked their heads and we headed back towards Ireland.

* * *

I have here beside me a snapshot that I think must have been taken that day. It has no date on it, but written in my mother's hand on the back the words 'Johnny and friend' and then an exclamation mark. The two young men stand with their backs to the sea. The sun must have been shining as Johnny's right eye is shut. He had the habit of doing this when the sun shone with reasonable brightness. His head is tilted slightly towards Bruno, almost resting on his friend's shoulder. Bruno is an inch or two taller than Johnny and he stands straight-backed and the sculpture of his curls makes him look even taller than he is. A cigarette droops from the corner of his mouth. They are both wearing bathing trunks and Johnny holds a towel in his left hand. They are grinning at the photographer, who I suppose must have been me, although I don't remember taking their picture that day. Their grins are towards me, but not for me. I realise now that the grins were indubitably for themselves.

I am constantly astonished by the fact that once you start to trawl through the waters of memory the strangest things get caught in your net.

Are they true or false these recollections that suddenly seem so clear in your mind? As I say I have no recollection of taking that snapshot but I have a vivid picture in my mind of the young men turning away from me and running into the sea, Bruno trailing a wisp of smoke from the cigarette that he still held between his lips. They swam straight out towards the horizon, till all I could see was the distant flicking of their arms.

I swam sedately up and down parallel to the shore and not too far out for safety. That is what I have always enjoyed, no-risk swimming. The water was still quite cold, and after a while I got out and dried myself and ran along the beach to warm up. I scanned the sea from time to time and could see no sign of them anywhere. I sat down with my back against a warm rock and stared out at the sparkling sea. The tide was coming in and the little boat that we had pulled up on to the sand now had water lapping at her keel. I didn't know how long it would be before she floated and had a little pain of anxiety inside me as I watched the water curl and uncurl, run and dance, always, inexorably, moving in across the sand. I became anxious and then a little angry, and when at last they came scrambling down the stony cliff at the back of the cove, laughing and catcalling and finally jumping down on to the sand, I burst into tears.

' 'Ello, 'ello, wot's all this, then?'

Johnny's funny voice.

My face was burning red, my nose stuffed with mucus. 'I didn't know where you were. I couldn't see you anywhere. I thought . . .'

'Silly, daft Im.'

'I thought . . . It's been so long. The tide . . . I thought . . .'

'You're behaving like a baby. You should know better. We can never drown. We are champion swimmers. We are—'

'Oh, shut up. You are a pair of mean pigs. I want to go home.'

I picked up my towel and togs and walked towards the boat, tears of anger streaming down my cheeks.

Steps followed me, a hand pulled at my arm. It was Bruno. 'Imogen. Just one moment, please.'

I pushed his hand away, but he took hold of my arm again. He pulled at me until I stopped walking and turned to look at him. Rippling water was now round our ankles. Johnny stood behind him on the dry sand, his hands on his hips, watching with a slightly exasperated look on his face. Bruno took my towel from me and, bending down, he wet it in the sea and squeezed it out. Then, most gently, he wiped my eyes and my scorching face.

'There,' he said, handing me the towel. 'That's better. Now blow your nose.' I obeyed. He took the towel from me and rinsed it carefully. He wiped my face again. 'We did not mean to be unkind.' His voice was low and very gentle. 'Please believe me. It was my fault. We could see this little path from the sea and I wanted to discover where it went. Up and up. It was so beautiful up there that we lingered.'

I remember smiling at his use of the word.

'Johnny is right. We would not drown. We are champions. Not in that sea.'

'Even a champion can come to a sticky end,' I said.

He laughed, and after a moment I laughed too.

[33]

'That is good,' he said. 'Come, we must get on the boat. Soon now she will be floating.' He put his hand on the back of my neck and we splashed towards the boat. One of his fingers moved up and down gently behind my ear; a good feeling.

'I also have a sister. She is the one person I miss. I would like her to be here with me, with us in Ireland.'

'How old is she?'

'She is one year and four days older than I am. That makes her twenty-one . . . We are almost like twins. You would like her. She, too, would like you.'

'I don't suppose so. I am only fifteen.'

'So?'

'She would think I am still a child.'

'I don't think age has anything to do with people liking each other or not.' We had reached the boat, which was now quivering like a living thing as the water began to raise it from the sand. He climbed on board and reached down his hand to pull me up. 'You have a very pretty name. Im-o-gen. It suits you well. You are a very pretty girl.'

I felt myself going red again. I was not yet old enough to accept compliments with calmness.

'Come, Johnny,' he called. 'Quickly, come, or we will leave you behind. Your sister and I will sail away forever and leave you here. Lonely.' He gave a sudden laugh. 'Jealous.' He glanced at me as he said the word; I pretended not to hear him.

Johnny clambered in and gestured to me to take the tiller again. 'I grovel, Im.' He pulled in the anchor that was now lying washed by the sea. He folded the rope neatly and we waited for the boat to lift from the bottom.

'Will we teach her to swim?' Bruno asked Johnny.

'I can swim.'

'Really swim,' said Bruno.

'I don't want to swim any better than I do. I just like being able to go up and down, up and down, and put my foot on the bottom if I want to.'

'Suit yourself,' said Johnny.

* * *

'Echo: a repetition of sounds, due to the reflection of the sound waves by some obstacle.' A down-to-earth and rather boring statement in the OED about a charming and somewhat romantic phenomenon.

If you stood in the garden of Paradise and shouted, the sound would swing back to you, pushed by the curving wall of the cliff on the other side of the bay.

'Yoohoo.'

Oooo . . . hoo . . . oo. The words skimmed the water like birds.

As a child I loved the echo. I used to stand on the lawn and sing, loud as I could manage, and the words would come back garbled, but recognisable to me, all plaited in on themselves.

'I want to be happy, but I can't be happy till I make you happy *toooo*.'

The answering echo seemed like a promise to me.

I used to wonder from time to time what the birds nesting on the cliff thought when they were bombarded with useless sound. When I asked my mother this question once, she gave me her smile and said nothing.

*   *   *

I sat on the edge of my bed in that expensive home for the mildly demented and thought about the things that no one would allow me to say.

I was no longer a child, according to the law, but I felt very little difference in myself at that moment from the child who was brought in speechless six months earlier.

Now I know a few more rules.

Perhaps, I thought, when you know all the rules, then you are truly grown-up. A laughable thought.

I was a child when they brought me in.

Children's perceptions of events are unsatisfactory.

The way children unravel mysteries is untrustworthy.

Children have poisonous imaginations.

So they say.

They said all those things to me.

I sat on the edge of that bed and thought these things over. I remembered that once I had been able to see things quite clearly, even during times of confusion, my mind could balance things, cope; I could understand the difference between truth and untruth.

My spoken truth.

When I came here first and began to speak again, I tried to speak the truth to them, the doctors, the nurses and those counsellors, and they confused me with their drugs and their spinning reasoning, until I began to question my own truth. But now, with Johnny's disappearance, I knew that my only madness was to think that they might have believed me in the first place.

Perhaps, I thought, I am now ready to become an adult. I now know when to lie.

'Daydreaming?'

It was the nurse again.

'You've let your tea get cold. What a girl you are for daydreaming. Eyes wide open, staring at nothing. That's over for now, time to get dressed.'

She picked up the cup of cold tea. 'I'll just run along to

the kitchen with this. I'll be back in five minutes, then we'll go and see Matron. You freshen up and get dressed, there's a good girl. Make yourself look fresh.'

She crackled out of the room.

I got up and went over to the basin. I looked at myself in the glass. To my eyes I looked quite fresh. I turned on the cold tap and slooshed water on to my face and rubbed at the back of my neck with my wet hands.

'Never put soap on your face,' Sylvia always used to say. 'It dries up your skin.'

I brushed my teeth.

'Always brush your teeth up and down, never across. It's bad for the enamel.'

I combed my hair.

'Always brush your hair a hundred strokes a day. It keeps it in good condition.'

I put on my jeans and a blue sweatshirt.

I combed my hair again.

By the time the nurse came back I was tying the laces of my trainers.

'That's a good girl. We'll go along so. Matron has a busy day ahead of her. Comings and goings. Today is filled with comings and goings.'

Matron's office was large and full of light. The garden stretched colourfully away outside the window. Chestnut leaves just starting to turn golden, the last roses red and white, and a gorgeous yellow in a bed beneath the window.

Matron was leafing through a pile of papers when I went into the room. She put down her pen and smiled. 'Imogen. Good morning to you.'

'Good morning.'

'You may go, Nurse. I'll give you a ring when I need you. Do come and sit down, my dear. Perhaps you'd like a cup of coffee? Nurse, would you ask them to bring us coffee?'

Nurse nodded and left the room.

The matron was dressed in a navy blouse and skirt with a small badge pinned approximately where her heart might be.

I sat down in a large leather chair that sighed when it took my weight.

'How are you feeling this morning?'

'I'm all right, thank you.'

'I would have come to see you yesterday evening, but I thought it better to let you sleep . . . to come to terms with . . . Dr Bailey told me the sad story. I can only say how very, very sorry I am. To lose a brother . . .' She sighed. She got up and went over to the window and looked out on to the sun-filled garden. I got the feeling as I watched that wherever she went in the world she would expect the sun to be shining.

'To lose someone so close to you . . . even when you are in your full health . . . even . . .' She looked at me in silence for a moment. 'I know. I do know. I speak from experience. My own dear brother was killed in a motor accident two years ago. I thought at the time . . . I speak now in confidence, you understand . . . My pain was so great that I thought I would not be able to . . . go on. I haven't said this to one other person. No. The pain was so . . . well, intense, life-threatening, it seemed to me that I . . .' She gave a sudden little laugh. 'Anyway, here I am. I'm just trying to say . . . I miss him. I really do miss him, don't think otherwise, but I have learned to keep my feelings to myself, and here I am.'

I wondered what she wanted me to say.

The door opened and a girl in a white dress came in with a tray . . .

'Put it on the table,' said the matron. 'Thank you.'

Without a word the girl put the tray down and left the room.

'I was able to fight all those feelings that threatened to drag me down. Right down. But then I was in my full health. You are fragile.'

She moved to the table and began to pour the coffee.

'Milk?' She held a silver jug poised over the cup.

I nodded.

'Sugar?'

'No, thank you.'

The matron carried the cup carefully across the room and put it down on a small table beside my chair. 'I always look forward to my morning coffee,' she said.

Her shoes were neat, black with a little gold strip let into each heel.

She poured her own coffee: a lot of milk and two lumps of sugar. She stirred it swiftly and sat down once more in her chair. She patted the file in front of her. 'I think you have made good progress. I hope, and your father also hopes, that this awful happening won't undo . . .'

She paused.

She took a sip from her cup. And then another.

She watched me like a hawk.

'No,' I said at last.

'No? What does no mean, dear?'

'Nothing will be undone. I can promise you that. Nothing. I am not any longer mad.'

She gave a little laugh. 'My dear girl, you were never mad.'

'Then why am I here?'

Her fingers riffled through the papers in front of her. ' "Emotionally very fragile" would be a better description. Not mad. You should never use the word "mad". '

'I think my mother thought I was mad.'

'No, no. You mustn't get that wrong. She felt you needed the protection of a place like this. You needed to recover your equilibrium. Yes.'

[41]

She looked pleased with her words. 'Yes,' she repeated.

We looked at each other across the desk, the neat piles of paper, undoubtedly all referring to others who also needed to recover their equilibrium, and the coffee cups. I wanted to laugh, but I had more sense. I had rediscovered sense. Were sense and equilibrium the same thing?

Matron had asked me a question and was leaning forward waiting for my reply.

'Sorry,' I said. 'I didn't quite catch . . .'

'Do you feel now that you could . . . cope . . . out there? Cope?'

'I would like to go home.'

'Of course, the fact that both your parents are doctors makes things much easier. I will speak to Dr McGuinness. We'll have to be guided by him, but I'm sure . . .'

'I am eighteen.' I said the words quietly, almost hoping that she wouldn't hear me.

Maybe she did, maybe she didn't. She rose to her feet. 'That's all, then. I have a busy day ahead. I will ring for Nurse.' She pressed a bell on her desk and the door opened as if by magic and the nurse was standing there. 'How splendid it will be,' said the matron. She smiled at me and sat down again, pulling some papers towards her.

'Thank you, Matron.'

I left the room.

* * *

To return for a moment to the notion of diary-keeping: my father's somewhat spasmodic entries seemed aimed at noting moments when he had behaved in a somewhat idiosyncratic manner and wished to be able to prove to himself at some future time that he had been right in his behaviour.

Today Johnny was three years old. As usual his birthday is celebrated here at Paradise. Now he has a sister of almost two months old and apparently thriving. How they can tell I do not know: she sleeps and feeds and squawks. This is all she has done since she came home from the hospital. The nurse tells us that she is thriving. The morning was warm and the sea like blue glass, quite smooth and glittering in the sun. I took Johnny down to the cove below the house, undressed him and, standing on the black rock from which we dive, I threw him into the sea. I have for a long time had the theory that small children, like small dogs, swim instinctively when unburdened by the anxieties and flapdoodles of adults. I was, of course, prepared to jump in after him if my theory did not prove correct.

The child was in no danger; I am a strong

swimmer. I was correct in my notion. He bobbed
up to the surface almost at once, being light in
weight, and began to paddle like a dog. I watched
for a moment, but saw no sign of distress. I dived
in beside him and gently nudged him towards the
shore, which was about twenty yards away. He was
cold when we came out on to the sand, shivering
in fact, and I wrapped a towel round him and
rubbed him dry and warm, telling him as I did so
how clever he was to be able to swim so well. He
never spoke. I gave him a piece of Bournville black
chocolate.

'We'll do it again tomorrow,' I said. 'One day
you will be a champion. Won't that be great?'

He didn't answer, presumably because he didn't
know the meaning of the word.

His body is so beautiful, like a small angel in a
medieval Italian painting.

Folded neatly between the two diary pages is a
newspaper cutting dated August 1967:

'Schoolboy Johnny Bailey takes yet another prize.
This junior goes from strength to strength. We can
only hope that the selectors have him in mind for
the next Olympic squad.'

And written in the narrow margin my father's triumphant YES!

The word 'bastard' sprang to my mind when I read this first, but now that I have struggled through all the papers in the trunk, I don't feel quite so vicious. I am also rather glad that I wasn't born a boy: I prefer to have been benignly neglected as a child rather than have the burden of other people's expectations heaped on my back. No one cared whether I could swim with both feet off the bottom, or was first or last in class, was beautiful or plain, friendless or the most popular girl in the school. I was unnoticed until I lost the power to speak.

I used to wonder why they'd bothered to have me.

I asked my mother that once, a silly thing to do, but at the age of sixteen it is difficult to avoid doing silly things. It is an age when you need to know that someone loves you. I had no such security. Sometimes I felt like a pane of glass: their indifference was so great that I felt they were unaware of my presence as I stood or sat between them.

I went into her study one evening; it was a small room half-way up the stairs. The one tall window looked out over the back garden; the walls were lined with books from floor to ceiling. She sat at her desk sorting case folders, presumably for the next day's clinic. 'Yes?' she said, without looking up from her work.

I didn't say a word.

After a moment or two she frowned and then looked up and towards me. 'Imogen,' she said.

'I am Imogen.'

I am so glad I never have to be sixteen again.

She sighed. She waved some papers at me. 'Can this wait?'

'No.'

She put the papers down on her desk and folded her hands. She didn't smile at me as I presume she smiled at her patients.

'Well? I'm listening.'

'I just wanted to know why you bothered to have me.'

'What?'

'Why you bothered to have me. You know . . . why you bothered.'

'What is all this about?'

'I know no other way to put it. Why you bothered—'

She held up a hand towards me like a policeman on point duty. 'I haven't time for this nonsense now, Imogen. We wanted another child, if that is an answer. We love you and care about you and worry and do all those things that parents do. Is that what this is really about? I shouldn't have to say this. At this moment I am very busy, so run along, there's a good girl, and we will discuss this when I have more time. At the weekend perhaps.'

The subject was never mentioned again.

✳ ✳ ✳

The shadows were long when we came up the field towards the house that evening after our day in the boat. I had recovered my equilibrium and we walked in step through the damp grass. Sylvia came out of the house above us and watched our approach.

' "There may be trouble ahead," ' sang Johnny softly, squeezing my arm close to his side. ' "But while there's music and moonlight and love and romance, let's face the music and dance." '

'Cole Porter,' said Bruno.

'*Dummkopf.* Irving Berlin.'

'Ach. I should have remembered.'

They both sang and all our feet cavorted.

Sylvia came down the steps towards us. We danced quite energetically. We held tightly on to each other's arms.

'You had me worried to bits. I saw no sign of you all day until about half an hour ago. Where were you? Why didn't you tell me you were not going to be here? You have no right, Johnny, to go off like that without a word. And lunch. I had the table laid and the salad made. And then only your father and I to eat it. You took the child. I called and called her name, and then I looked in her room and she had gone without making her bed. How could you all be so thoughtless?'

Johnny dropped my hand and moved towards Sylvia. 'Darling Mutti. Mutti, *liebchen* . . .'

Bruno put an arm round my shoulders and I could feel him vibrating with silent laughter.

'. . . do forgive us. It was rotten of us. We should have had a carrier pigeon with us and we could have released it with a message tied to its little leg. "Dearest Mutti, unlay the table, scrap the salad, It is too perfect to come ashore. Wish you were here." ' He knelt at her feet, hands clasped.

'Get up. Get up, Johnny. You are too absurd. You have been drinking. I get the whiff from you. I hope you haven't been giving the child drink.'

'Would I?'

Bruno let go of me and went up the steps towards her. 'Madame . . .'

'Mr Schlegel, I hold you responsible. You are old enough to have a bit of sense. What would your mother say in the circumstances?'

He shook his head.

'Alas, Madame, my mother is . . .' He paused delicately. 'I have not had the benefit of a mother's care for long years, so you must forgive my lack of thought towards you. I do hope, though, that you might, perhaps, give us the pleasure of your company tomorrow when we sail. Then you will understand how we could have been so negligent today.'

He turned and stretched out both arms towards the sea. 'It was like a wonderful dream. Like Paradise. Your house is so aptly named. To be out there was to forget everything. So . . . please . . . tomorrow . . . to make the day even more perfect . . .'

My mother blushed.

Johnny put his head down and dashed into the house.

'How very sweet of you, Mr Schlegel.'

'Please, Madame, my name is Bruno.'

'Bruno. I'd like that very much. It's such a long time since I've been out sailing. Three years, four, perhaps. Johnny usually goes with his father. I'd like that very much indeed. Imogen can get her father's lunch and I can have a whole day free.'

Bugger them all, I thought.

Bruno took Sylvia's hand in his and kissed it. 'Are we forgiven?'

'Of course you are.'

'Can't I come too?' I asked.

'Someone has to see to your father.'

'We could leave his lunch ready for him.'

'That's enough, Imogen. Now go and tidy up. Dinner is ready.'

I turned and walked away down the hill. 'Rotten,' I shouted, across the water.

Otten.

ott . . . e . . . en.

Sylvia went back into the house with Bruno by her side.

'Rotten,' called Johnny from his bedroom window, but softly so that only I could hear.

* * *

The papers smell with age and lack of affection; folded letters have yellowed and crumbled; the bold black ink strokes and curves have become pale and, where the folds have been, quite indecipherable. In a brown envelope with a couple of letters I found a stiff piece of parchment, freckled with brown age spots. It was headed in gold.

BUCKINGHAM PALACE
I join with my grateful people
in sending you this memorial
of a brave life given for others
in the Great War.

It looked like a gaudily dressed poem; some laureate's attempt to mourn with mothers and fathers the loss of their son; but it was merely a king's distant acknowledgement, like a wave of a gloved hand, of some sort of heroism. Not even a scrawled signature in his own hand, a stamped 'George RI'.

Rex Imperator.

So much for heroism!

In the same envelope there was a real poem, scratched by my great-grandmother on a black-edged card,

There in the lull of midnight gentle arms
Lifted him slowly down the slopes of death,
Lest he should hear again the mad alarms
Of battle, dying moans and painful breath.

And where the earth was soft for flowers we made
A grave for him that he might better rest.
So, spring shall come and leave it sweet arrayed,
And there the lark shall turn her dewy nest.

Francis Ledwidge (also dead before his time)

and then pages torn from a notebook, folded and refolded to fit into the envelope, probably untouched since the words were written.

Sometimes when I look in the glass I see nothing.
No, that is not quite true, I see the room in which I
stand or sit, the chairs, tables, my mother's
escritoire, the curtains tied back with their silk
tassels, books, pictures, the cushions sometimes

quite orderly, other times pressed and tossed by the
weight of living people; I do not see myself, that is
what I mean to say.

I do not see myself.

Sometimes.

Other times I see myself and wish that I could not.
The last four years have drained me of energy, beauty,
style. I know in my head that we have to order
ourselves to continue to lead life as we know it should
be lived, but my heart disallows me. I live in a state of
distracted melancholy.

Patrick is so strong: he holds the family
together, he acts as mother and father to the
children, though they are, of course, at an age now
when they no longer need the comfort of a
mother's warm embrace.

I keep the house ordered, that is a duty that I feel I
must perform, and I play the piano. I have even set to
music some of the poems of Francis Ledwidge and I
sing these when the house is empty. If I open all the
doors, up and down these high stairways into every
room, I like to think of my voice wandering through the
house, lingering in one room or another, unmolested by
the laughter and boisterous chat of living people. Still,
when I hear the hall door open, I wait to hear Harry's
voice.

'I'm home Mama.' He always shouted those words, even after he stopped being a child.

Dear God, when was that? He moved from one uniform into another at such speed that we were all left breathless.

He died on his nineteenth birthday.

A neat trick of God.

His commanding officer said that he died well. I do not know what this means.

This day is his birthday.

He would have been twenty-three today, had it not also been his deathday. We would have celebrated as usual down in Paradise, with a picnic and swimming and then dancing in the evening for all the family and local friends. It will be almost autumn down there and the chestnut leaves will be starting to yellow.

I have not been down there since the day we got the telegram. Patrick has tried to persuade me to go with him but I have not the energy to make the long journey and wrestle with the grief that I know would be waiting for me.

Here, the young men are dying also. We hear the gunfire at night and see the tenders full of uniformed men rattling down the streets. We read in the papers of atrocities and counter-atrocities.

People all through the country are afraid to go out at night. I have to say that I am glad that Gerald has chosen to go to Cambridge. I would hate to have him here getting mixed up possibly in what is happening.

I have never understood why men choose war rather than peace. People smile when I ask such questions and treat me as if I were dim in the head. Even men of God don't seem to want to explain such things to me.

The dimness, of course, is not in my head, it is now and will be for ever in my heart.

✳ ✳ ✳

There is no sign of any of her music among the papers; maybe she never wrote it down, it just flowed from her head through her fingers and then round the empty rooms of that house, and her voice singing to emptiness the melancholic words of Francis Ledwidge. I have loved her piano so much since I read those pages of hers. Alas, I have only her long, arrogant nose and not her musical facility.

✳ ✳ ✳

I watched them sail off the next morning. Johnny at the tiller, Bruno and Sylvia chatting to each other in the bow. I waved from my window, but no one waved back. I went back to bed. I sulked all day, not that it mattered very much: only my father was around and he never seemed to notice what sort of a mood I was in. He read the paper while he ate the lunch I had prepared for him, from time to time making little grunts of either anger or amusement, it was hard to tell which. After he had drained the last drops from his coffee cup he looked at me for the first time. 'Does Johnny talk to you?'

I didn't know what to say.

I said nothing.

He stared at me, the fingers of his left hand tapping on the folded 'Irish Times' by his plate. He cleared his throat.

'I had a most extraordinary conversation with him last night. After dinner. Quite late, actually.'

My father had the habit of sitting late in the drawing room with the windows wide open, listening to music. He loved sixteenth- and seventeenth-century church music, and if I wasn't sleeping I could hear the sounds of Palestrina, Thomas Tallis, Monteverdi drifting up through the night air.

'I am only mentioning this as I thought that maybe your brother had spoken to you on the subject.'

I waited for a long time before he spoke again.

'He told me last night . . . He came in his pyjamas and told me . . . I was listening to Monteverdi, *"Salve O Regina"*. Yes. And he came in and spoke. I had to turn the music off.' His voice was peevish. 'He told me that he wants to give up his swimming.'

I was startled. 'He what?'

'He wants to give up his swimming. He has made up his mind. There was no arguing with him.'

'But why?'

'He wants to concentrate on his school work. Pass his Leaving with flying colours. He's afraid . . .'

'Johnny's never been afraid of anything.'

'. . . the intensive training to get on to the national squad might interfere with his academic work.'

'But . . .'

He held up his hand. 'I could not persuade him. His mind is made up. I have to say that I am disappointed. Bitterly. Yes. I wondered if perhaps he had spoken to you about this.'

I shook my head.

'Brothers and sisters . . .' he said.

I continued to shake my head.

He sighed. 'I haven't told your mother yet, so don't say a word.'

A little laugh escaped through my mouth. As if, I thought. As bloody if.

He frowned slightly as if he had heard my thoughts. 'I think you misunderstand your mother.' he said. 'A lot of girls of your age have problems with their mothers. It's part of the process.'

I got up and began to clear the table, carrying the dishes over to the sink, turning on the hot tap, squeezing large quantities of mild green Fairy Liquid into the swirling water, which she never let me do.

'What process?' I asked.

'The process of growing up, of course.'

'Maybe that's what Johnny is doing too.'

'He tells me he has spoken to the head. I really feel he should have spoken to me about this before he took irrevocable steps. I myself will speak to the head the moment we get back to Dublin. He should think of the honour for the school, if nothing else. Perhaps even the country. Johnny . . . and I . . . well, I had such . . . I have invested so much time and energy in promoting . . . I . . . had hopes.'

I turned the tap off and faced him. 'He did say something to me once.'

'And? Yes. Yes.'

'It was last year and he said that his swimming coach was a dirty old bugger who kept feeling up his private parts.'

My father went bright red. I turned back to the

washing-up. 'Imogen! How dare you? How – I don't believe a word … That man … that man, and I know him personally. I personally asked him to take Johnny on for extra coaching. He is a most respected and highly respectable man. Highly. Married, Imogen, with several children. And the best coach in Ireland. I made it my business to find out. I simply do not believe that Johnny said any such thing. You are a mischief-maker. I won't listen to any more of such nonsense.'

I heard his chair scrape on the kitchen floor as he got up.

'I am shocked, shocked, Imogen. How could Johnny have said such a thing to a child? I do not—'

'Believe it or not, he said it, and as you said yourself I'm growing up and all children know about dirty old men, these days. We need to know.'

He walked swiftly out of the room and slammed the door.

'They exist,' I shouted after him.

* * *

I don't suppose he ever mentioned that conversation to Sylvia: they never seemed to talk all that much with each other. They had their separate lives, their separate friends, their separate rooms. Johnny and I were the only tenuous threads that ran between them. Maybe it's the same with all marriages, to a greater or lesser degree. I don't know. I've never put my head in that noose.

I was not then, nor have I ever been, a mischief-maker. His words made me cry . . . after he had left the room, of course.

I stood by the sink in the kitchen, and as I cried, the sun caught in the budding branches of a chestnut tree bathed me in its warmth.

*   *   *

There are letters in the trunk from all over the English-speaking world. My ancestors might have been adventurous but they were not linguists. Maybe, of course, they were not even adventurous, just driven by some kind of fear to leave this country in the twenties and early thirties.

My great-grandfather must have watched with dismay the slow leaching out and away of all his children bar two, my grandfather, Arthur, and my great-aunt Millie, who never married and lived with her father from the time of her mother's death until he died in 1927, three years after my father was born.

While Arthur was a pillar of society, hard-working, high-minded and a man of great charity, Millie seems to have been a thorn in the family's flesh. Suffragism, socialism, vegetarianism, atheism, and a great desire to pass as much of her father's money as she could get hold of to the poor were the motors that drove her life. She used to spend her summers walking the roads of the Irish Free State, as it had then become, accompanied by a large Alsatian dog, sleeping in ditches and hay barns and occasional police cells, if the weather was bad, doling out florins and half-crowns and good dietary advice where she felt it was needed. The winters she spent at Paradise, herself and the dog in the small maid's bedroom behind the kitchen, where she used to write tracts, which she would hand out on her journeys, on pacifism, socialism and how to feed yourself and your family from the local hedgerows and woods. My father used to tell me stories about her when I was a small child, his voice full, as he spoke, of unusual affection. I never quite worked out if he was encouraging me to be like her, or warning me against it. Sylvia disapproved of such stories. Scornful and unamused, she said to me one evening after my father had left the room, 'Don't pay too much attention to your father's fairy tales. She was a crazy creature. She should have been put in a home, for her own safety. Thank God there's not too many of her kind loose in the country these days.'

I have always loved the thought of her and I have, no doubt, sanctified her inside my head, while not wanting in any way to emulate her lifestyle.

I am too fond of hot water, soft pillows, books, good

food and wine to follow her along her principled path, no matter how much I may admire her. My father admired her. I like him for that.

I actually grew to like him quite a lot after Sylvia's death in 1983. He became mellow, smiled from time to time and seemed pleased to see me when I visited. Sometimes he would take my hand and hold it for a few moments between both his hands. Then he would squeeze my fingers, sigh and let go. I always felt he was thinking of Johnny at such moments, but maybe not. Maybe I have always been paranoid about his feeling for Johnny.

He remained on in that big red-brick house in Lansdowne Road, high granite steps to the hall door and the quiet footsteps of ghosts moving across the Turkey carpets. He played the piano and listened to music and gave small dinner parties from time to time for his male friends. I was never invited. He always seemed pleased when I called in, but never made any moves of his own to see me. After Mathilde's death in hospital, a quiet middle-aged man called Gregory moved into the house and remained with my father until his death. In fact, he was sitting by the old man when he died last year, and when I came into the bedroom he looked up at me with such sorrow in his face that I threw my arms around him and pressed him to me, longing for a moment to share his love.

Love is so hard to find and I was so glad at that moment to discover that maybe my father had found it.

* * *

10.8.15

Dear Father,

We have been fighting now for more than 4 days and I am sorry to say have lost most of the Btn. We were doing fatigues for the first 2 days and only lost about 10 men but yesterday morning about 3 a.m. we were called up to stop a counter-attack. In about 2 hours we lost 12 officers and about 450 men. How I got through I shall never understand, the shrapnel and bullets were coming down like hail. Three men were shot handing me messages. The Colonel also got through all right. Luke had his hand blown off but is all right. Martin got a slight wound in his arm. In the last 5 nights I have had about 5 hours sleep but still feel fairly fit in body but my heart is broken for all those fellows that I liked so much. The water here is very scarce. We get one qt. per day to do everything with, cook, wash etc. I am at present watching the 2 Divisions which are coming up getting the most awful shelling. We are at present much nearer to the enemy than they are, but they are giving us a rest. When they come up we will all attack.

After yesterday I have a feeling I shall get through this 'job'. I would like to see some of the young lads who are staying at home get a few days of this. If they weren't killed they would or should die of shame.

I must shut up as I have a great deal to do before this show starts.

Give my love to Mother and everybody at home. I hope you are well. So long. I have not had a mail yet.

Thanks ever so much for all you have done for me.

Yours as ever, Harry

On the back in neat black writing:

Letter recv'd from my son Harry Bailey, written in the mountains above Suvla Bay and recv'd by me on 20th August, five days after his death. We recv'd the news of his death by telegraph on 18th August 1915.

I have not shown this letter to Louisa as her state of desolation and grief is so great that I fear the sight of Harry's handwriting might be too much for her sanity. I have to bear in my mind constantly the thought that we are not the only people in this city to be suffering such terrible loss. This is such a small country; it is intolerable to think of the young men who marched out of this city so recently and to realise that so many of them will never come back, and the others who will return maimed in body and soul. I should never have allowed either of the boys to go. I should have heeded Louisa and exerted my parental authority, but after the recent trouble with Harry and the possibility of future intolerable scandal brought on the whole family, I felt that perhaps he might purge his sin by going to fight for his country. Having made this decision in my head I could not in all conscience have allowed him to go and not Arthur, who has always let his mind linger on the thought of being a soldier rather than following me and so many of my family to the bar. I pray for forgiveness for not holding to my principle and for Arthur to return to us unharmed and for God to be more forgiving towards my boy Harry than man could ever be.

I have tried to persuade Louisa to come with me to Paradise for a few weeks, but the notion drives her into more floods of tears, so we must stay here in these dusty summer streets where sorrow hangs in the air. I know she fears most terrible that the second telegraph will come, but I have a little hope and must hold on to that.

The second telegram never came. I am the living proof of that.

I wondered as I read my great-grandfather's note what the trouble with Harry had been that had made him write with such anxiety the words 'intolerable scandal'.

* * *

They came silently up the hill from the jetty.

I watched them from my bedroom window: first came Johnny with the picnic gear and the life-jackets that no one ever wore hefted across his shoulder. He looked a little glum, I thought, sun-baked but glum. That made me a bit pleased.

I wondered as I watched him what Father might have to say to him on the subject of the swimming coach. Probably nothing: he would have persuaded himself that my words were merely mischievous, and he would say nothing, either to Johnny or to Sylvia.

Bruno and Sylvia walked twenty or so yards behind him. They came out of the darkness of the trees, her arm through his as if she needed for a while his support, their bodies leaning close together. As they walked he talked quietly, bending down towards her. I heard the sound of her laughter. I felt an ugly rage in my body and I drew back from the window in case they might spot me and in some way see my mood and mock me for it.

I heard Johnny running up the stairs and called out to him, but he went past my room to his own door, which he opened and then slammed behind him.

My mother and Bruno laughed in the garden just below my window. My mother was not a woman to whom laughter came all that easily but at that moment she sounded as if she were.

I went downstairs after a while and found Bruno and Sylvia in the kitchen. He was at the sink washing leaves for a salad; she was sitting at the table sipping at a glass of white wine.

'Where's Johnny?' I asked.

Bruno turned round and smiled at me.

'I sent him to his room. He was being tiresome,' said Sylvia. 'You know the way he can be tiresome. Cheeky.' Her face was pink with sun and tiny particles of salt and sand glittered on her cheeks.

'Poor Johnny. Can I have a glass of wine?'

She frowned and shook her head, but Bruno flapped the water from his hands, took a glass from the press and put it on the table.

'She is after all fifteen,' he said to my mother. 'At home everyone has a little glass by the age of fifteen.' He poured some wine into the glass. He pushed it across the table to me and winked, a sort of secret drooping of the eye.

'Thank you.'

Sylvia did not object.

'Did you have a good day?'

'Perfect. It is such a pity that the holiday is now at an end. It would be good to continue with such days.' He was back at the sink as he spoke, shaking the leaves in the colander.

Johnny did not appear for dinner. I suggested that I should bring him up some food on a tray, but Sylvia shook her head again, and this time Bruno minded his own business.

I lay in bed later that night and listened to the night sounds, the distant bark of a fox, the creaking floorboards, an owl hooting as it flapped across the field below the house, the soft whispers from the room next door and a little burst of surprising laughter from Johnny, quickly stifled, and always the sound I love best in the world, the constant sighing of the sea.

* * *

I find that child Imogen difficult: difficult to understand, difficult to talk to, difficult even to be alone in a room with. She stares at me from time to time, expecting something. If she could tell me what she expects maybe things would be different, better. I suppose that I as the senior person in this relationship must be to blame. I don't like this, I have never liked being the one to blame.

I have never had such problems with Johnny, but maybe I have been fooling myself. Until now I always thought that all was well between us, that we had the same dreams in our heads. I no longer feel this. He treated me last night with extraordinary contempt, as if I knew nothing, either about him or about the world.

Is there really what they call a generation gap? I have never believed so up till now. I was a dutiful son; I hope that I have been a loving and concerned father. It seems now I could have expended all that energy on something else, pursued my interest in baroque music, travelled the world. Becoming a champion swimmer is not one of his dreams. 'Follow your star, Johnny,' I said to him. 'Swim for Ireland. After that is over the other things will fall into place.'

He smiled quite politely at me. 'If you'll forgive me for saying so, Father, I seem to have been following your star all these years. I was blinded by it. Now I can see.' He gave a funny little bow and left the room. I have not yet spoken to Sylvia about this, nor do I think I will.

I do not like this German fellow. I don't know why I have written this down, but I just feel I must. I think he smiles too much, but that, of course, is a brainless reason for not liking him. I think maybe he is behind Johnny's decision, not necessarily to give up swimming but to outface me.

* * *

I never have been able to understand why my parents continued to live in that unwieldy house in Lansdowne Road. I suppose my father had some morose affection for the home in which he had spent all his life, and Sylvia was the sort of person who really didn't care where she lived as long as it was waterproof, warm and trouble-free. She had no desire to modernise, to put her stamp on things, to lighten up the dark rooms in any way. Their one concession to the modern way of living was to turn the large stone-floored basement into a flat and install there Mathilde, an apparently devout Catholic lady from Prague, who had come to Ireland not long after the war and had remained believing it to be the closest country in the world to God. My mother had helped her with work permits and immigration problems and eventually her naturalisation papers, and Mathilde had lived with us and cherished us until three weeks before her death in 1992, when she was discovered to have advanced cancer of the lungs and died in a private room in St Vincent's hospital, surrounded by flowers and visited twice daily by both my father and myself. I missed her from my life far more than I ever missed my mother. I still miss the warmth of her embrace, her chocolate cake, and her great capacity for listening, even to the most terrible rubbish. She, I know, will be waiting at that great gate to welcome each one of us in, with chocolate cake and warm middle-European kisses. I hope that Johnny is aware of this wherever he may be.

Every time I hear Mozart being played, I think, with warmth in my heart, of Mathilde.

The house was not big in terms of the number of rooms but cumbersome and, as I have said, quite dark. My great-grandmother's piano sat in the back part of the drawing room. Father played on it in the evenings, practising certain phrases over and over again until sometimes I thought I would go mad. It was kept meticulously in tune by a man from Pigott's who came four times a year; after he had finished the tuning he would descend into the basement and have tea and chocolate cake with Mathilde.

She didn't like Bruno.

When he came to Lansdowne Road for a meal, or sometimes even to spend the weekend, my father, never the most talkative of men, would retreat into almost total silence and Mathilde would retreat into the basement, appearing only when totally necessary. Her lips would become thin and tight when he was around, and her eyes never looked in his direction. He pretended not to notice but I think he was irked by her attitude. He used to try to charm her by bringing her little presents, a rose, a tiny handsewn lawn handkerchief or chocolates wrapped in gold paper and tied with ribbon. She would plait her fingers together in front of her and smile a thin, cold smile. 'No presents,' she would say, and leave the room, her shoes squeaking softly.

I asked her once why she treated him in this way, a way that seemed to be quite against all her loving instincts.

'I do not like Germans,' she said. 'And I do not have to tell you why, Miss Curiosity Kill the Cat.'

That was that. No use to argue with Mathilde when she spoke with such vehemence.

I used to wish that she did like him, so that I could sit in her kitchen, surrounded by the wonderful smells of strudel and simmering soup, and tell her how I loved him.

I needed someone to whom to speak that secret. She had her own secrets, like all of us, but, of course, when you are sixteen years old you think you are the only person in the world who has things and thoughts to hide.

I would like to describe the house at this moment, in case the recollection of it might lure Johnny to return, to stand perhaps at the granite gatepost and stare at the red-brick walls and the bowed windows and remember that there had been good times and there might well be again here in this city that has changed so much over the last twenty years: though you might recognise this street, you might no longer recognise the attitudes of the people who live here. The house is some sort of government department now and the holly bushes and the flowerbeds that used to bloom in front of Mathilde's windows have gone to make way for a tarred car park. The granite steps up to the hall door glitter in the sun as they always used to do. The hall door is recessed into a porch and, as in the old days, our old days, the knocker, the bellpush and the letter-box gleam with polishing.

Of course, the inside will be unrecognisable, but that doesn't matter, Johnny: your memory can get to work on that and, in the way that we all recover the past when we need to, your recollection will be as true to you as mine is to me.

I am happy to be a rooted person: I hated my months

of so-called madness and when I came out of the home and went back to live for a while in my parents' house I swore that never again would I allow myself to fall into such darkness, I would hold hard to equilibrium. I really want no adventures in my life, except, of course, the challenges I create for myself in my own head.

I think quite frequently about my great-grandmother. I presume it must be from this woman with the long nose that I received the gift of creativity. I have to be grateful for that, although maybe my life would have been simpler if I had felt able to opt for those warmer commitments, marriage, children, nest-building. I am not grumbling, merely musing, not drowning, merely waving.

※ ※ ※

Here is another of her tightly folded messages. She, of course, was drowning.

*I lie awake in the darkness of the curfewed night and
hear from time to time running footsteps in the
street below. Sometimes the light from a Crossley
tender sweeps my ceiling as it turns into the street
and for a moment my heart seems to stop as I fear for
the owner of the running feet. I imagine him crouched
in a doorway, hiding from the searching light, and*

*I think to myself as I lie tense in my comfortable
bed, Another young life will be destroyed. I also
wonder what would have happened if Harry had
survived the war. Would they have sent him over
here to subdue his fellow countrymen? If so, how
would he have borne such a burden, and how
would he have continued to live here after all this is
over? It will be over. I know that. We all know
that. Everything will in the end be changed, but it
will all be over.*

*Why that the naked poor and mangled peace,
Dear nurse of arts, plenties and joyful births,
Should not in this best garden of the world put up her lovely visage?*

*This makes me smile a moment when I remember all
those joyful births.*

*Joy and smiles are so alien to me now: I feel I am
diseased and may contaminate the healthy family
around me, my dear Arthur and Gerald and the girls.
I feel I must shut myself away from them for their
own safety. I cannot share their pleasures and I must
not inflict pain or disturb the equilibrium of their
youth.*

*I think I may well be mad. I see that in Patrick's
eyes when he looks at me. He himself is so ebullient,*

*so full of the will to live a rich life, that he fails
to understand how very fragile humans can be. I
have been very happy with him; I do hope he realises
that.*

*I have music in my head, but somehow the energy
to draw it down into my fingers does not exist any
longer. Maybe the energy to breathe will not exist for
very long, either.*

* * *

We never went to Paradise for Christmas.

Cities are the places to spend Christmas: busy streets, shops, bars, restaurants sparkle and glitter with lights and the heightened excitement of fiesta time. In suburban streets curtains normally pulled for privacy remain open to show the glow of firelit rooms and trees hung with gaily coloured lights.

Our house had a tall tree in the front bay window of the drawing room, a small tree in the window of Mathilde's sitting room, and then in every other window a tall red candle flickered from dusk until the following morning light. Holly, ivy and mistletoe, swagged and clustered, little bunches of lights hung like flowers from the green branches and every vase and bowl in the house seemed to be filled with chrysanthemums, yellow and gold and red and white. Sylvia's notion of what Christmas should be like was meticulously old-fashioned, as was Mathilde's, and the smells of her scrumptious cooking pervaded the house from top to bottom: spices, herbs, simmering winy sauces and chocolate all blended with the smells from the chrysanthemums and the needles that slithered from time to time from the tree. We were all wrapped in pleasurable anticipation. It was hard not to smile each time you came into the hall. Here was safety and possibly love. It was always the same; I remember snow once or twice, but otherwise all recollections of Christmas are, in my head, one delightful collective memory.

But that Christmas, the last one before our family fell apart: I remember that Christmas because I was seventeen and I was in love with Bruno and I believed that he was in love with me. He did not go back to Germany for Christmas that year as he had done for the two previous years.

'Would it please you, Imogen, if I stayed in Dublin for Christmas?'

We were coming home from a concert at the Royal Dublin Society; he always insisted on walking the short half-mile to my door with me. A cold winter night with a wind blowing the dust up from the street into my face and a million stars like hard sparking stones in the sky. I had been watching the breath pulsing from his mouth as he spoke.

'Imogen?'

'I . . . oh, yes, of course. How perfectly splendid that would be.' I gave a little hop of pleasure and then remembered that I was no longer a child: I had to keep control over my feet, my giddy hands, my bony elbows, calm these extremities of mine, make sure that I had them under control.

'But what about your family? Your mother, won't she mind?' He shook his head.

'But I thought Christmas in Germany was so . . . well . . . familial?'

'Alas.' He paused for so long after the word that I thought he wasn't going to speak again. 'My mother is not well, Imogen. It is a long time now since she has been well.'

'But . . .'

He held up his hand.

'There is no point,' he said. 'My sister tells me in her letters that there is no point. My mother has no longer any idea who she is or where she is. So what is the point? my sister says. What is the point?'

I thought about this as we walked. I thought about not knowing, not understanding. What would a touch, a gesture, a smile mean to someone who knew nothing, who floated in some sort of limbo? 'How does she know?' I asked him.

'Know what?'

'How does your sister know this? Maybe there is

something there that she has missed. Maybe she only appears not to know. That could be the reality. She just can't express how much she knows.'

'You don't know what you're talking about.'

'That's true enough. I just . . .'

'She has senility. First-rate doctors, not only just my sister, but first-rate doctors have assessed her. She lives now in a home for demented people.'

'How sad.'

'She is well cared-for. My sister sees her monthly. She sees to everything, she watches over her well-being. I send her flowers for important dates. I do not wish to see her myself. I like only to remember her the way she was until last year. She is no longer my mother.'

I didn't like that idea much. 'She can't be very old.'

'No matter her age. I have no longer a mother.'

'I don't think you should say things like that.'

He touched the side of my face with his fingers. 'Sweet Imogen,' he said.

My face was cold, his fingers warm. I felt their warmth sink down into my body. I felt I might cry with joy. I didn't want to say a word in case my voice might tremble as I spoke. The wind seemed to whip his fingers away and the warmth went with them.

'It is about Christmas we talk,' he said. 'Not my family affairs. Not my private feelings.'

I said nothing.

'If you do not like that I should stay here, of course I will not do such a thing. What you feel is important to me.'

We turned right into Lansdowne Road. Two minutes and I would be home.

'So say something.'

'Yes,' I said. 'I would like you to stay here.'

'Good. That is settled then. I will speak to Johnny. I will ask him to ask your mother if I may celebrate Christmas Day with you all.'

'I'll ask her. I'm sure she will be delighted.'

'No. Johnny is the one to ask her.'

'I . . .'

'I think it would be better.'

I nodded. 'Whatever you think.'

'Sweet Imogen.' He touched my face again, just a light brush with his warm fingers. 'There you are. Home. In you go, quick, out of this cold wind.'

He turned and walked away, back the way we had come, and I stood and watched him striding in and out of the pools of light and the moving shadows of the bare branches.

It was at dinner a couple of nights later that Johnny asked Sylvia. Mathilde had just carried in the aromatic leg of lamb and my father was feeling the edge of the carving knife with his thumb.

'Bruno can't go home for Christmas.'

'Blunt.' My father reached for the whetstone. 'Why can no one in this house sharpen a knife?' He began to rotate the edge gently on the stone.

'Why not?' Sylvia asked Johnny.

'Only me. It's always left to me.'

Grnngrnngrnn.

'Some sort of family problem.'

Grrnnn.

My teeth ached.

'It is quite impossible to carve if you don't have a sharp knife, Mathilde.'

Mathilde looked cross. 'You know very well, Doctor, that only you can sharp the knives to your own satisfaction.'

Grrnn grrnnn.

'You are, after all, a surgeon,' said Sylvia. 'A professional carver.'

I laughed, half to stop my teeth aching and half because I felt it was needed.

'I just wondered if perhaps he could come here for Christmas?'

'Bruno?'

'Yes.'

Whick, whick, whick.

'I don't see why not.'

'At least I don't have to sharpen knives in the theatre.'

Whick. He ran his thumb along the blade again and sighed.

'He'd better come and stay for a couple of days,' said Sylvia.

'Who's that?' asked my father, starting to carve the meat.

'Bruno.'

'Oh, God,' said my father. 'When is this visitation to happen?'

'Christmas. He can't go home. He will be all on his own.'

'Has he no other friends to leech off?'

'That is unkind.'

'I will not like to cook Christmas dinner for a German,' said Mathilde, unhelpfully.

I laughed again.

'What's to laugh?'

'She presumes you're joking,' said Sylvia.

'I am not making a joke. I will cook this fellow's dinner because he will be your guest, but I will not like to do it. That is no joke. See?'

'Why don't we eat before the food gets cold?' asked my father.

Mathilde tramped out of the room and banged the door.

* * *

Boxing Day/St Stephen's Day, 1969

I always smile to myself on this day, mainly because Christmas is over and also because of the split in my head about the name of this day. I have been brought up to call it Boxing Day . . . I've never had enough curiosity to discover what the name means, perhaps just the day on which we dispose of all the boxes our unspeakable presents came in; now, not so much boxes as gaudy wrappings and coloured ribbons and labels with spurious messages written on them . . . See what a grouch Christmas Day has made me! The other name, of course, being its Christian name, used by and large by everyone in this Christian country, except for a few ageing and recalcitrant people like myself whose parents would have had a leaning towards things English and therefore not very Christian. I tend to think Boxing Day and say St Stephen's Day just so I won't get sneered at by friends who take such matters seriously.

The child Imogen gave me a recording of some Bach cantatas and as I write I am listening to the counter-tenor singing the measured and angelic notes of '*Es ekelt mir mehr zu leben*'. Of all voices

that is to me the most perfect. I must remember to
thank her properly for her thoughtful gift.

The German continued to smile. He bought us
all extravagant presents. I did not buy him
anything as I consider that three days' food and
drink is present enough. Mathilde, I notice, has left
his present to her unopened under the tree. Sylvia
will not like this: I sometimes get the feeling that if
she felt she could manage her life without
Mathilde she would send her packing. I also get
the feeling sometimes that if she could manage her
life without me she would send me packing too.
No such luck, I whisper to myself, when I have
this notion in my head. No such luck. If I were at
Paradise this moment I would run like a child into
the garden and shout: 'No such luck.' And the
echo would agree with me.

Clarinet, flute and harpsichord finish up the
piece now. Tidy, orderly and reasonably joyful. I
like that. I like the lack of excess. I do not like that
German. Excuse me. I should not write such
things in my diary. I should keep such thoughts
hidden. Something written even in secret is no
longer hidden.

* * *

Slight dusting of snow; as usual too late for Christmas.

' "The north wind doth blow and we shall have snow and what will the robin do then, poor thing?" ' I sang. I stood by the window and watched the miserable flakes being twisted in circles by the wind.

'Do shut up, Im, some people have work to do.'

'You've become a real swot since you went to college.'

'There are so many books to read, stuff to take in. If you remember, I got out of the way of working at school.'

'Books, books, books. Moan, moan, moan. Will you never have fun again? Does fun end so quickly?'

'Silly question.' He bent his head to his book again.

I went back to staring at the snow.

Post-Christmas lethargy wrapped the house in silence. Bruno had gone, Johnny would go back to college tomorrow, Father and Sylvia had gone to lunch with some friends and Mathilde was, no doubt, busying herself with something in the basement. She never sat still; if she did sit, she had sewing in her hand, darning or neatly patching triangular tears in the old linen sheets, matching little pearl buttons, searching in her sewing box for the right implement or coloured thread, squinting towards the light as she threaded her needle and always humming little snatches of songs, jiggly unfinished musical phrases that just seemed to bubble up unbidden from the centre of her body.

Bruno had kissed me under the mistletoe just before he left that morning. With one hand he had held the back of my head and he had nibbled my lips with his soft lips and touched the inside of my mouth with his tongue. I gasped when he did that and he let go of me at once and stepped away. Sylvia had at that moment come out of her study and stood at the bend of the stairs. He laughed and held his hand out towards her.

'This is my moment for goodbyes. Come down, Sylvia, and let me kiss you goodbye.'

She came slowly down the stairs and he stood at the bottom with his hand outstretched. Johnny leaned against the drawing-room door and watched. As Sylvia reached the bottom of the stairs she put her hand into Bruno's. He bent and kissed it and then taking her gently by the shoulders he pulled her under the mistletoe and kissed first her left cheek and then the right.

'Goodbye,' he almost whispered.

'Au revoir, Bruno,' she said.

'And me,' said Johnny. 'Johnny wants a kiss too.'

He spoke in a baby voice and we all laughed.

'Naughty Johnny.' Bruno put out a hand and ran his thumb along Johnny's cheekbone, catching a wisp of hair and smoothing it back behind his ear. Then he was gone, almost like magic; the hall door was shut behind him and I could hear his feet running down the steps and then the slamming of his car door. For a few moments no one spoke.

'Well,' Sylvia had said at last. 'Christmas is over.' She went back up the stairs and into her study.

' "He'll sit in the barn and keep himself warm and hide his head under his wing, poor thing." ' I sang the words aloud.

Johnny sighed. 'Im!'

'Sorry. Couldn't you talk to me for a while? Here we are alone. It's simply ages since we've been alone. I forget—'

'Forget what?' He dropped his book on the floor and came over to me. He put an arm around my shoulders and hugged me. 'Forget what?'

'I forget how long it's been. A year? An age. It seems like an age.'

'Life becomes so different when you leave school. I'm sorry.'

'Am I too foolish for you? Boring? I'm still me. I'm getting older too. How long do I have to wait for us to be pals again?'

He laughed. 'You're such an ass, Im. "Pals" is such a silly word. Old-fashioned. No one uses words like that any more. Not here, anyway. Maybe in England. Jolly good pals. That sort of stuff. I'm just chock-a-block with new things happening. New people, new emotions. I'm not too sure about this law thing. Maybe I'm not cut out to be a lawyer. What do you think?'

'What do you mean "new emotions"?'

He didn't answer.

'Johnny?'

'Do you think I'm cut out to be a lawyer?'

'It's in your genes, my learned friend, just skipped a generation. Better than being a chartered accountant.'

'That hadn't occurred to me.'

'Or a doctor. I can't see you as a doctor at all. You're not all that interested in people, are you? Perhaps you should have stuck with the swimming, become a national hero and then made a fortune after it was all over signing people's bathing togs and smiling. A doddle.'

He laughed again.

'What do you mean "new emotions"?'

'Curiosity killed the cat.'

'You've fallen in love with someone. Johnny, what fun. Who is she? I'd love to meet her. Is she pretty? Do let me meet her. I promise, truly promise, that I won't say a word.'

He took his hand from my shoulder and went back to his chair. He picked his book up from the floor. 'God, you can be so tiresome. So bloody girly.' He opened the book. 'Sorry. I have to get on.'

'You've got all evening to swot.'

'I'm going out.'

'And leaving me on my own with them. Thank you very much. Where are you going? Are you meeting her?'

'I'm going for a drink with Bruno. Now, can you please shut up?'

'You know that Mathilde has left her present under the tree?'

'Yes.'

'Sylvia says it's very rude of her.'

'Yes.'

'Why?'

'Why what?'

'Why is she so . . . why doesn't she like him?'

'How am I expected to know the workings of Mathilde's mind?'

'No . . . but . . . she's so great . . . so, well, you know, great. She likes people. She's kind and Mathilde. So very Mathilde.'

'Im . . .'

'How can she not like him?'

'Why don't you ask her?'

'She wouldn't tell me. She'd just push her shoulders up and down and make a funny face.'

'She doesn't like Germans.'

'But . . .'

'But me no buts, *kleine Schwester*. He's a German. She doesn't like Germans. QED.'

'But why?'

'Do I have to give you a history lesson?'

'It's just so unlike Mathilde to be unkind and rude.'

'Think gas chambers.'

'But . . .'

'Deportations, camps, Kristallnacht . . .'

I put my fingers in my ears and yelled at him, 'I am not listening. Not listening.'

He began to read his book again, but I could see his mouth working, hear through my fingers the words he was saying.

'Forced labour, experiments on babies, *Juden' raus* . . .'

I threw myself on him and began to pummel him. He just caught my wrists and held me as he used to do when we were children. He always used to win.

'He is not like that. All that has nothing to do with him. Anyway Mathilde is not a—'

'What is this hullabaloo?' Mathilde caught hold of my shoulders and pulled me away from Johnny. 'What is this? Is it not possible to sit at peace in this house without you two hullabalooing? What age do you think you are?'

She stood behind me, holding me, her warm hands gripping my arms. 'You have been teasing her? Pulling her legs? You know she has no stomach for such happenings. You are bad, Johnny. And you.' She shook me gently and then let go of me. 'You know she has no stomach for teasing.'

Johnny laughed. 'I'm sorry, Mathilde. I wasn't teasing her, I promise. I was just jogging her memory on the subject of twentieth-century history.'

'You give me a heart-attack. I have to come running up those stairs to stop you fighting. When you stop being children?'

'You could just let us fight.'

'No. I am in charge here when your parents are not in. I will have no fighting. I do not like fighting.'

I realised that I was crying.

'Wipe your face, Imogen. You are too old now for a runny nose and weeping eyes.'

I pulled a tissue out of my pocket and did as I was told.

'Now,' said Mathilde. 'What was that all about?'

Johnny said nothing.

'I'm waiting.'

'He said you were a Jew.'

'I never . . .'

'Well? So? If I am?'

'You're not. You go to Mass. You have a statue of the Infant of Prague in your bedroom. You bless yourself when you pass a church. You're in the Legion of Mary.'

She laughed. A dry laugh, unlike her usual rambunctious one. 'And so it is a reason for you to cry and hit your brother because he says I am a Jew.'

'Oh, no, Mathilde. I didn't mean that. It was Bruno . . .'

'The German? You cry about the German?'

I felt my face getting red. I thought that at any moment I might cry again.

'He is not worth to cry about.'

She was looking past me at Johnny as she spoke.

'But,' I said, 'how can you be—'

'Imogen, you could not, not ever, understand. I pray to God, if there is a God, that you will never have to understand. I have no people left who ever knew what I was and what I am now. I hide. I hide since I was a girl, since I walk out of that camp in 1945, I hide in the manners of others. My disguise is in the belief of others, the protocols, the reverences. I am a coward, Imogen. I don't want to stand out in a crowd because of my beliefs. I want to hide in the crowd. I want to be invisible, for ever. So, it was so simple to me. When I decide to come to Ireland I decide to become a Catholic and no one until now has questioned this. So, you see, my Imogen, you have put the cat among my very private pigeons.'

I began to cry again.

She produced a large handkerchief from a pocket and handed it to me. 'Don't cry, don't cry. There is no fault. No blame. No need for crying.'

I threw my arms around her and howled on to her shoulder. She held me tight and hushed and crooned as if I were a baby and she were my loving mother. 'This is better,' she said at last. 'Much, much better.'

Johnny got up from his chair and stood beside us, looking a little lost. She put out an arm and pulled him into our embrace. 'We are three people now with a secret. That makes us perhaps a kind of family, no?'

'Yes, Mathilde.' We both spoke at the same time. We both pressed ourselves into the warmth of her body. Then, as suddenly as it had all started, it was over.

'Look,' she said. 'My sleeve it is all wet with your crying. Wipe your face, my girl. You look like a sight.'

She took the handkerchief from my hand and scrubbed at my face.

'Now, on about our business. My cake will burn and then I can tell you there will be blame. You will wash your face before your mother comes home.' She walked to the door, then turned round and smiled at us. 'When you have lost everyone you love,' she said, 'it is quite hard ever to be normal again.'

'Don't you love us, Mathilde?' I asked her.

'You are my family now. Of course I love you but you are not my own.' She lifted her hands in the air and made a comical face. 'My cake. Jesus, Mary and Joseph, with all this nonsense my cake will burn.'

We laughed and she disappeared. Johnny took my hand and held it to his face for a moment. Neither of us spoke a word.

* * *

I left the Home to go home a few days after my interview with the matron. The nurse helped me pack my clothes and my books into a brown leather suitcase, which must have belonged to my grandfather Arthur as his initials, AFB, were placed obliquely across the right-hand corner of the lid. I have no idea what the initial F stands for. There was a faint smell when the lid was raised, of other people's clothes, mustiness and dead air.

I pushed the top down and Nurse snapped shut the locks. 'It's well for you,' she said. She was wearing pale green crackling cotton that day.

'What?'

'Going home so soon. Back to Mammy and Daddy.'

She must have remembered my father's last visit and the news he brought because she went red in the face. 'You'll be a comfort to them,' she said.

'I doubt it.'

She slapped me playfully on the arm. 'Bad girl, don't say things like that.'

'No. I suppose I shouldn't.'

'You must behave.'

'Yes.'

'You wouldn't want to find yourself back in here again.'

'No.'

'Nice and all as we are.'

'Nice and all as you are.'

'I'll miss you,' she said. 'It's a lift to have young people around the place.'

I laughed.

'Don't get me wrong,' she said.

A cloud passed across the sun and the room was grey for a few moments.

Nurse sighed. 'You can get on with your life now. I'd like to be your age again.'

'You're not old.'

'I'm not young. I'm stuck in a rut. I feel I'll be here until it's too late to do anything else.'

'Do you wear contact lenses?'

Nurse looked surprised. 'Yeah,' she said.

'I've noticed. Your eyes always match your clothes. I like that. I think that's brave. I don't think you'll be stuck in a rut. I don't think that anyone who does that sort of thing will ever be stuck in a rut. I'll never have the energy to do anything like that.'

'I never know if anyone notices. I put them in in the

morning and I look at myself and I wonder if I'm a little touched. Ready for the funny farm.' She went red in the face again. 'Listen to me.' She gave a nervous giggle. 'Can't keep my big mouth shut. Miss Foot In Mouth, my dad always calls me. Maybe I'll go to England. I've a sister in Birmingham. I might go and join her. You have all your life in front of you.'

I looked at the calendar on the wall beside my bed: all those crossed-out days, all that silence and sleep and the spurious news of Johnny's death.

'I will find him,' I said aloud, and the nurse laid her fingers lightly on my shoulder and said, 'Imogen,' in a warning voice.

'Accept,' she said to me. 'You have to learn to accept. That's what the world's about, really.'

'I'll bear that in mind.'

That was quite rude of me, I realised, so I leaned forward and kissed her, then picked up my case and started on my way home, to normality. 'Thanks,' I said, as I left the room. 'You've been great. I hope things work out for you.'

Sylvia had sent a taxi for me: it was one of her clinic days. The driver was sour-faced and I climbed silently into the back. The matron and the nurse stood just outside the front door and the wind blew their skirts sideways as they waved goodbye.

The wind was also blowing when we arrived in Lansdowne Road. Mathilde ran down the steps to kiss me and pay the driver and kiss me again and clutch at my arm and kiss me half-way up the steps, and her face was red with emotion and the coldness of the wind, and her grey hair was trying to escape from its prison of nets and hairpins and was tugging and twisting in its efforts to be free.

We arrived eventually at the hall door and she pushed it shut behind us and kissed me again.

The house was calm and quiet.

The grandfather clock opposite the dining room door ticked its deep pulses; I was suddenly aware that I had never consciously heard the sound before, and probably never would again. It was such a pleasant sound to welcome me home.

It went when I sold the house. No one has a place these days for a grandfather clock, no one has patience to wind it, no one wishes any longer to be reminded regularly of the passing of time. I regret now having sold it. I remember now the comfort I found that day in its measured beat.

'You are thin,' said Mathilde, her voice full of worry.

'I'm all right. It's good to be thin.'

'Too thin.' She pushed me towards the back of the hall, towards the stairs down into her flat. 'Leave your case there. I have tea ready for you. I have chocolate cake and apple strudel. I have not made apple strudel since you went away.

What did they feed you? It was not as good, I fear, as what you get at home. I wanted and wished to send you food, but your mother said no. I said why no? And she said that we must leave you alone to get well. What harm, I said to her, is there in chocolate cake? My chocolate cake is cooked to make people happy and what Imogen needs at these moments is to be made happy. But she says no, and who am I to argue with your mother?'

A huge fire crackled in the grate and Mathilde, not drawing breath, pushed me down into an armchair. 'Sit. Be like you always were, child, curled up in that chair like a pussy cat. You must be the same again only you mustn't take things so hard. That was always your problem. You took things too hard. Too serious. I said that to your mother and the doctor. I said, "here you are, two doctors, and yet you can't see that all that is wrong with that child is she takes things too hard." In the old days doctors used to see that sort of thing. You were never mad, Imogen. Mind you, I'm not so sure that everyone else was not a little mad. And then Johnny . . .'

She put a cup of tea down beside me and I saw that her hand was shaking. I put out my hand and took hers. 'Mathilde. He is not dead. He's run away. Somewhere in the world he is alive.'

She shook her head. 'No, no, no, no.'

She took a handkerchief from her pocket and blew her

nose. 'No,' she said again. She looked at me with anger. 'You must not say such things, Imogen. You are now the only one that I have left in the world and you must not say such things. They can take you away again.' She smiled suddenly at me. 'It may be true what you say, but you must not say it. For me. For Mathilde, keep your mouth buttoned.'

'I'm grown-up now, Mathilde, they can't do that to me again. But I won't say a word. I've learned that. I'm dying for a piece of chocolate cake.'

✢   ✢   ✢

Arthur was married three days ago in St Anne's Church in Dawson Street. Helena's parents, who farm in Tipperary, had been made aware of the fragility of my health. Indeed, I believe that Patrick had said that I would be unable to travel such a distance to the wedding and so they most kindly agreed that the service should be held in our parish church.
I pulled myself together and, with the help of the girls, I saw to not only my own clothes but also to their bridesmaids' dresses . . . a most unbecoming shade of pink, chosen by the bride, with little caps made of silk rose petals. Helena seems a nice girl and I'm sure that she and Arthur will be as happy as can be, but her taste in clothes is abysmal.

Millie, being Millie, refused to be a bridesmaid and
gave the excuse that it was her duty to look after me. I
think she made this decision after having seen the
colour the dresses were to be! I was glad to have her at
my side. Patrick said I looked quite my old self. I have
to say that I had chosen for myself a most becoming
blue silk toque with a charming veil. 'Rather royal,'
Millie pronounced, but she smiled as she said it, which
I presume meant that she thought it suited me. The sun
shone and the day was warm. We walked from the
church the few hundred yards to the Shelbourne Hotel
where we drank champagne and chattered and the
young people danced and looked so beautiful. It seemed
so easy for those few hours to forget the world and its
sorrows. It was the next morning that we heard the
news of General Collins's death and I realised that as
we had been dancing he had been dying. More than he,
of course, have died and will die and die. There have
been little skirmishes in the streets near here and we
have heard gunfire from the direction of Stephen's
Green. I try to keep the girls indoors, but it is
impossible to reason with them. They mock me and
then kiss me with great affection, put on their hats and
go to meet their friends. In a day or two they will go
down to Paradise for the remainder of the summer and
I will be alone. This week has leached away the energy

that I had built up, so I will be glad of the quiet and the half-pulled curtains and the sighing memories. I have just read a charming poem of Ledwidge, which I will set to music and sing while they are all away.

> *He will not come, and still I wait.*
> *He whistles at another gate*
> *Where angels listen. Ah, I know*
> *He will not come, yet if I go*
> *How shall I know he did not pass*
> *Barefooted in the flowery grass.*
>
> *The moon leans on one silver horn*
> *Above the silhouettes of morn,*
> *And from their nest-sills finches whistle*
> *Or stooping pluck the downy thistle*
> *How is the morn so gay and fair*
> *Without his whistling in its air?*
>
> *The world is calling, I must go.*
> *How shall I know he did not pass*
> *Barefooted in the shining grass?*

The first notes sing in my head. One, two, three, four. That is all at the moment. One, two, three, four. He will not come.

A little tremor in my head, that is all at the
moment, but more notes will come, either trickle or
cascade; like the first drops of rain on your skin before
the downpour happens. I will wait hands outstretched
to catch the drops as they fall.

I know if I stay alone in this house he will be here.
He will hear my singing as he passes up and down the
stairs.

✳ ✳ ✳

I remember throwing myself on my bed, full of chocolate
cake and apple strudel, and just lying there happy to be, for
a moment, free. Mathilde had put flowers on my dressing-
table, the window was open and the smell of autumn
rustled in with the breeze. Someone down the road was
cutting grass and a child called and then laughed and then
was silent.

Such old and faithful and friendly things salve you, I
thought, and then wondered if there were such a word; my
books, pillows, an old blue silk eiderdown and curtains that
tremble slightly at the open window. My dressing-gown
hung on the back of the door, my great-grandmother's
silver hairbrush with her ornate initials sat as it had always
done slightly to the right of centre on my dressing-table.

I will have to leave here, I thought.

Soon.

Not too much shilly-shallying, not too much sinking into this morass of comfort and anger. Not too much of Mathilde's love and Sylvia's indifference. Father was too predictable: he would just agree with Sylvia in whatever decisions she took. I didn't want to have people making decisions for me: the one they had made on my behalf, earlier in the year had nearly finished me off and had possibly been instrumental in finishing Johnny off too.

'Yoohoo, Johnny,' I called, but there was no echo here. The walls and the curtains absorbed the sound.

* * *

The moment I saw my mother later that evening I thought I was going to lose my voice again. I stood on the landing outside my bedroom door and she came up the stairs towards me, silhouetted against the long window and the garden and the falling, glinting rays of the sun going down behind the trees. She had called to me from the hall, and the door had slammed behind her voice. I heard her footsteps on the stairs. She continued to call my name: 'Imogen. Imogen. Imogen.'

I went out on to the landing and her black figure ran up towards me. I reached out and switched on the light and she became herself, dressed in green with a red scarf, her hair neat and curling, and a smile that was both welcoming and reluctant. One hand was stretched out towards me. I remembered at that moment that in her mind I was her only living child. Then I thought that I had lost my voice. I took a step towards her and she took my hand then pulled me into an embrace.

It was so unlike Mathilde's warm, soft, new-bread hug that I almost wanted to laugh, but I didn't and we stood angled into each other in silence and then she said, 'Welcome home, darling.'

I couldn't find my voice anywhere so I smiled.

She pushed me away, keeping one hand on my shoulder and looked me up and down. 'You look well.'

She didn't. Her face was pale, almost grey, and she had huge black rings under her eyes.

'I'm so glad you look well. Thin but well.' She gave a little stuttering laugh. 'Mathilde will fatten you up soon enough.'

I surprised myself by the word that eventually came out of my mouth. 'Mother,' I said. I didn't remember ever having called her that before.

She stood very still for a moment. 'Yes,' she said. 'That is what I am.'

*   *   *

Sylvia called me into her study one evening about a week after I had come home. She was sitting at her desk filling up a form of some sort. 'Just a tick,' she said. 'There's so much paperwork these days. Sit down.'

I sat down opposite her and waited.

She frowned, crossed something out and wrote something else in tiny writing on the form. She signed it and put it to one side.

'I've spoken to the head.' She tapped her pen on the desk.

'The head what?' I asked.

'Your head. Miss Baker.'

'Oh.'

We looked at each other in silence.

'My ex-head, you mean.'

'She has agreed to take you back. You can re-do last year and have a stab at your Leaving. If you work hard you shouldn't have a problem . . . but if you don't get decent grades we can think about a crammer for next year.'

There was another long silence. She picked up her pen and tapped it on the desk again.

'No,' I said at last.

Someone had to say something.

'I don't think—'

'No.'

'We have decided. Your father and I—'

'No.' I stood up. 'I became eighteen when I was in there. You know what that means. I can now make my decisions for myself. I am not going back to school.'

'You must finish your education. You're in no fit state to make decisions of this sort.'

'Why not?'

'You—'

'I have been discharged. I am not mad. I am well. I am fit. I have been thinking a lot.'

The door opened and my father put his head round. 'Ah, there you are. It's almost time for dinner. Ah, Imogen, I hope you had a good day.' He waved a hand in my direction.

'She's being tiresome,' said Sylvia.

'So soon?'

'She says she won't go back to school.'

'Why don't we talk about it at dinner? We don't want to upset Mathilde.' He held out his hand towards me and I took it. We walked down the stairs hand in hand; an unusual occurrence. Sylvia pattered behind us. His hand was warm and quite dry, his skin almost like paper.

The dining room had red flock wallpaper and one of those brass lamps over the table with a red silk shade that you could raise or lower at will; it hung permanently at head level, so our food and the table settings were brightly illuminated and our bodies were in shadow; our hands, like disembodied creatures, moved in and out of the light, cutting, buttering, scooping and generally manipulating.

From the darkness Sylvia repeated her words. 'She says she won't go back to school.'

There was a long silence as my father chewed his mouthful of goulash. 'Hmmmm,' he said, at last.

I watched his hands. They laid his knife and fork neatly down and then positioned themselves on the table, one on each side of his plate; the first finger of his left hand tapped rhythmically on the polished mahogany.

In front of my mother her food was untouched, the knives and silver sat in their neat arrangement on the table.

I ate. I was hungry all the time for the comfortable food that I had not been offered for so many months. Anyway, I felt, whether I ate or not was unlikely to affect the decision that was about to be made.

'Hmmm,' he said again. 'Have you a reason?' he asked me politely.

'Edward . . .'

He raised his hand ever so slightly from the table and gestured towards her. 'Sylvia. Please. I have asked Imogen a question.'

I shut my eyes. It seemed easier to speak in that blackness where there was nothing to distract me and make the words stumble as they came out of my mouth. I didn't want to sound uncouth in any way, so darkness was best. 'I should have left school in the summer. I should by now have my exam results. I should be about to start in college. Through no fault of my own . . .' I paused both to think how I should phrase neatly my next words and also to find out if either of them would speak. They remained silent.

'Through no fault of my own I am sitting here and you seem to be expecting me to take a step backwards in my life. No, is what I say. I make no apologies for being blunt. I am not mad. They told me so before I left that place. I have never been mad, in spite of what you two may believe, and I am now eighteen and therefore able to make my own decisions. I am not going back to school.'

'This is ridiculous. She must go back to school, Edward. I have discussed this with Miss Baker. She is certain that this would be the right way forward for Imogen. She will accommodate us in any way possible. We must not delay with arguments and battles. The sooner Imogen returns to normal the better.'

'Maybe, of course,' he said, 'she no longer wishes to go to university. If this is so, it changes the picture.'

I opened my eyes. Father's hands picked up his knife and fork and began to push food around on the plate.

Sylvia spoke. 'It is too important a decision for her to

take, after all she has been through. Think, Imogen, think. Your whole future may depend on this . . . Edward . . .'

His hand lifted his fork up into the darkness where his mouth was. He said nothing.

'I am not going backwards. I really can't do that. I feel as if I have wasted a lot of time. I want to start my life.'

'You are being nonsensical. Stubborn. Edward.'

'I really have very little to say.' The fork clattered down on to the plate again. He picked up his napkin and dabbed at his chin. 'Your mother has looked after your education so far. Has made the decisions. I gather from her that you have done well at school. I think perhaps you should listen to her. She knows more about . . .' He stopped speaking and gave a little cough. 'Let's just say that I was not very successful in dealing with Johnny and his problems.'

'Edward.' Sylvia's voice was angry.

'Anyway', I said. 'Whatever.'

I packed some more food on to my fork and put it into my mouth.

'And what does that mean?' asked Sylvia.

'It means that whatever you want I won't do, so you can fuck off. That's what it means.'

'I don't think we need that sort of language,' said my father.

'I think we do. I like it. I like to say "fuck". It makes me happy inside to say it. I'm going to be a new person from now on. I'll probably say things like "fuck" quite a lot. If I feel like it. So.'

Father and I ate in silence for a few minutes. Sylvia didn't move. I could hear music from Mathilde's radio drifting up through the floor, some operatic aria, I think it was.

'I don't intend to stay here long. I'm not going to cadge money from you. I have that thousand pounds that Godfather left me and I would like, if I may, to go down to Paradise and live for a while in Aunt Millie's shed.'

'A thousand pounds won't last you very long.'

Mother began to eat after she had spoken the words.

'I intend to get a job.'

'Washing up? Babysitting? Shop assistant?'

'Whatever.'

'We're thinking of selling Paradise. Your father has been mulling it over in his mind.'

'Well, I can be useful, then. I can show people round it, keep it clean, that sort of thing.'

'You'll be lonely there all on your own.' My father sounded concerned.

'No. I really look forward to being on my own for a while. Please, Father, let me do this.'

I heard him sigh. 'I do intend to sell the place. I don't

have much heart for going down there again. You understand what I mean?'

'Yes. But it may take a while to sell. I could . . .'

'Yes,' he said. 'I see no reason why you shouldn't do that.'

'Edward, you never think before you speak.' She leaned towards him and her face was lit by the pale light from the lamp. The hollows beneath her eyes were like dark caves.

At that moment I stopped hating her. Mind you, I didn't start to love her, but at that moment to stop hating seemed enough. I felt a light dizziness in my head, like soda water, I thought, like soda water: that's what it was like to be released from hate, nothing more profound than soda water. I shovelled some more food into my mouth.

'On the contrary,' my father was saying, 'I think a lot, my dear, and speak little. I would have thought you would be aware of that.'

'The child's health. The child's future.'

'As she has pointed out, she is no longer a child. She can do as she wishes. I think the best thing we can do is try to smooth her path. Yes. Smooth her path. I'm sure you agree.'

'She has never looked after herself.'

'Perhaps it is time she tried.'

'Her illness . . .'

I got fed up. 'I'm here,' I said.

Total silence fell on us, during which I finished up the food on my plate.

'I love Mathilde's goulash. I want to live on my own. I want to find out what sort of life I want to live. I'm sorry if this upsets your plans for me, Sylvia. I don't apologise to you, Father, because I don't suppose you have any plans for me. I can maybe now begin to educate myself. I have my thousand pounds; it may not be a fortune, but maybe it will tide me over until I find out what I want to do. Maybe I will be a shop girl, or a street sweeper or a waitress, but I think you both owe it to me after the last months to let me work out the course of my own life. I don't want to live here or to go to college or to be given the gift of a suitable job by one of your kind friends.' I took a deep breath. I hadn't spoken so much in many months: the back of my throat felt exhausted. 'I feel blank,' I said. 'A huge blank white wall. Something quite unstarted. I want to start. What will I do with this wall? What? I have to find that out. I'd like to start into that as soon as possible.'

I wanted to say that I thought that was what Johnny would be doing wherever he was, but good sense told me not to. I stood up. 'I'm tired. I have found the last few days tiring. Even after eight months the world seems to have changed. Trying to catch up is tiring. I'm going to bed. Tomorrow things will be clearer. I will let you know my plans then.'

'Aren't you going to have any pudding?' asked my mother. 'Mathilde will be upset.'

The door behind me opened and Mathilde swept into the room, carrying a large empty tray. 'Mathilde will not be upset,' she said, laying the tray on the sideboard and beginning to rattle plates and dishes on to it. 'Mathilde is upset for sadness, not for people who don't finish their plates. She is tired, that child. She must go to her bed. I will bring her pudding to her in bed and a little glass of *porto*.' She paused for a moment. 'Medicinal.'

Father laughed. 'Oh, Mathilde, how could we ever live without you?'

'You couldn't. Run along, Imogen. Have a nice hot bath and then I will arrive. Scoot.'

* * *

The country is now at peace, but so many hearts have been broken and so much bitterness has taken root in men's minds that it will take a long, long time for trust to grow between those who once were comrades with a single cause and then became bitter enemies. So many of our friends and family have drifted away to England or the colonies, wanting to assure some sort of future for themselves and their families. Patrick sighs and

then laughs and calls them fools. 'This is an infernal
bloody country,' he said to me the other day, 'but it's
my infernal bloody country and I hope my children
feel the same about it. For better or for worse. It's like
a marriage.'

I thought sadly as he said those words about our
marriage, and how my debilitating illness had
stolen the charm and attachment that once we had.
They say that the grief I felt, and indeed still do feel
over Harry's death, depleted my body's capacity to keep
healthy to such a degree that it may take me many
more years to recover. What they don't realize is that I
do not want to recover . . . which, of course, they
would consider to be a form of madness. Maybe it is. I
find I cannot forgive Patrick for the fact that it was at
his insistence that Harry joined up. I know this for
sure, though Patrick has never spoken of it to me. I
know more about this whole miserable affair than he
has seen fit to tell me. I am not a fool and I most
bitterly resent that both he and Arthur have conspired
to keep me in some sort of darkness about it. I am sure
this is for the best and most gentle of reasons but I am
perhaps not a very reasonable person and I sometimes
hate them for it.

But to better news. Here we are in some sort of
peace and Arthur and Helen have produced a son.

Helen came round this morning with the little baby in order that I should see him in all his glory. She came straight from the nursing home in Hatch Street in Arthur's new motor and flew up the stairs with him clutched in her arms and laid him in my lap. 'Isn't he most beautiful?'

'The lucky baby has my nose.' I laughed as I said it, but my heart felt a great heaviness. It was as if Harry had been placed in my lap. Not just the same long nose, but a tiny wisp of hair fell towards his forehead and he opened his dark newly born eyes and seemed to stare at me. I touched his hand with a finger and he uncurled his fingers and clutched me.

'We are thinking of calling him Harry. Would you be pleased with that?'

I shook my head.

'Father-in-law thinks it would be a nice idea.'

'Please, no. I could never bear to speak, to call out to him. If you wouldn't mind. No.'

She is a sweet girl and she touched my shoulder gently. 'Edward is our second choice.'

'I can live with Edward.'

I felt churlish after I had said those words, but the dear girl seemed to understand and smiled at me, then leaned towards the baby on my knee and said gently, 'Edward, lovely Edward.'

*New world. I want a new world for this child. I
have lived for over half a century in the old one and I
do not like it.*

At one of those dances we went to that Christmas, Johnny
and Bruno and I, out somewhere Killiney way, I wore a new
red silk dress and he said I looked so beautiful that I would
have to sit in the front of the car beside him, instead of
being relegated to the back as I usually was when I was with
the pair of them.

'Oh, God, yuck,' said Johnny. 'We are being the little
gentleman tonight.'

'It's very icy,' called Sylvia, from the hall door. 'Mind
how you go.'

Bruno turned from the car and bowed towards her.

It was a starry night with a great white moon, clear and
hard, hanging above us, its reflection in the frozen puddles
along the road, in the dark windows of the houses, and
then larger than I had ever seen it before in the black, still
sea. I remember that I didn't want the drive to end: it was
as if we were driving away from the earth, drawn by the
magnetism of the moon. I wanted to drive to the moon. I
knew that for the moon I was unsuitably dressed in my red
silk dress and new, red leather strappy sandals, specially for
glamour but too high for safety. I would surely break an
ankle on the moon. My great claim to fame; the first

woman to break an ankle on the moon. Potentates and presidents would send me their condolences when I arrived back on earth, still in my red silk dress.

What fun.

What silliness.

The car stopped under a leafless tree in the driveway of a house bursting with light and voices and music.

Not the moon, no cold glacial solitude.

The door opened and Johnny hauled me out.

The ground was sparkling and slippy. Johnny held tight on to my arm. 'You'll break your leg in those silly shoes,' he said, 'Beautiful, Im, but quite daft to wear on a night like this. I'm amazed Mathilde let you out in them. You're actually looking quite grown-up. Isn't she, Bruno?'

'She is grown-up.' Bruno took my other arm. 'I will look after her this evening. You go and play with your friends, Johnny. I will mind Imogen.'

Johnny laughed.

'Babysitting?'

'I don't hear when you say things like that.'

Johnny held out a hand towards Bruno. '*Geb' mir.*'

'*Ich habe nichts.*'

'*Geb mir*, Bruno.'

'What the hell are you two going on about?'

'None of your business, Im.'

'I'm here standing between you both. You're being so

rude. I pretty well hate it when you go on like this. And I'm not a baby.'

Bruno pressed my arm tight against his side. He put his hand into his pocket and brought out a small black box.

'*Danke schön.*' Johnny took it from him. He hit Bruno lightly on the shoulder. 'Be good.' He put the box into his pocket and ran up the steps and through the open front door.

'What was that?'

'Let's go in. You must be frozen. Let's go and dance, Imogen. I wish to dance all night with you.'

It was warm in the hall. The house smelt of food and drink and laughter. I was cross with them both. I felt I should go home, but the smell of laughter was always so enjoyable and his hand was holding my arm deftly just above the elbow, warm and deft. His breath was in my hair. 'What was it?' I asked again.

'A box of dreams. Let me get you a drink.'

'You can't put dreams in a box.'

'Or will we dance first?'

'I hate people keeping secrets from me.'

'You'll have a hard life then. Everyone has secrets.'

He pulled me into the room where people were dancing, lights down low, and old, old smoochy music playing. He put both his arms around me and held me very tight. We swayed and swirled. I thought of dreams. If I were to keep dreams in a box, it would be a silver box studded with gaudy jewels. Yes. And the tissues of my dreams I would fold carefully, smoothly, and press them down into the safety of my silver box. And when I took them out they would float in the breeze, swaying and swirling, multicoloured. Alive for a while.

The music stopped and we stood there unmoving and the unknown dancers laughed and talked, disturbing the darkness.

'Don't move,' he whispered into my hair.

' "The Cloths of Heaven".'

'Excuse?'

' "The blue and the dim and the dark cloths". It's a poem we learned at school, about dreams.'

'I am only dreaming about you.'

No one had ever said such a thing to me before. 'Yeats,' I said, not knowing what else to say.

'*Ja*.'

The music began again, more of the same. The music of someone's parents, I thought, and we began to dance once more.

We were together all evening: we danced and drank glasses of red wine and sat on cushions in a corner and he talked about his childhood in Germany and swimming in the Baltic Sea and about his father who had lost a leg in the war and had become an alcoholic and would sit all day with the curtains pulled, drinking and listening to Beethoven, until he died at the age of forty-two filled with rage and grief, and no one had missed him after he was gone.

He kissed me and then we danced again and then there was Johnny, standing in the shadows watching us, his eyes glittering as if lit by lasers inside his head. As we danced past him he put out his hand and took Bruno's arm. We stopped beside him.

'So?'

'It's time to go and you haven't danced with me yet.'

Bruno laughed. 'I am happy with Imogen. Why should I dance with you?'

'I have no one.'

Bruno put a hand on the back of Johnny's neck and said something in German that I couldn't hear. Johnny threw his head back and laughed. Then he put an arm round each of us and swung us into the middle of the floor.

We clutched at each other for support, arms, shoulders, Bruno's hand on the back of my neck, Johnny's head thrown back. 'Good night, ladies, good night, ladies, good night, ladies. It's time to say good night. Time, time to . . . time to . . . and, gentlemen, it's time to say good night.'

Abruptly he stopped swinging and we stood in the middle of the floor, our heads spinning, and he bowed to the other dancers.

'It's time to say good night and good fucking.'

Someone clapped. Johnny pulled us from the room.

'That's all it is, of course,' he said, as we went down the steps, 'that sort of party, a preliminary to fucking. Or being fucked. I'm sitting in the front this time.'

He opened the car door and got in. All the way home he and Bruno spoke German to each other in what sounded like angry whispers.

When we got to Lansdowne Road they both got out of the car, both walked up the steps with me and then each in turn kissed me on the cheek and the evening was over.

* * *

When I told Mathilde that I was going down to live alone in Paradise she nodded. 'Is good. There is a good place for you to live. A healing place. Some day I will come down and visit you there.'

'That would be lovely. Please do that.'

She never was able to. I was there for a short couple of months and then the house was sold and I had to move from Millie's shed into a one-and-a-half-room flat in Cork City. It didn't bother me. I had got a job sub-editing on the 'Cork Examiner', and it was handier being in the city. I would fall into bed at four thirty in the morning and fall out again early in the afternoon, and I enjoyed the buzz of people in the streets and shops and the possibility of making friends of my own and sustaining those friendships in my own way and at my own speed.

Mathilde used to send me food parcels, as if I were living in some third-world country and in possible danger of starvation: wonderful rich fruit cake, neatly packed boxes of shortbread, half a dozen oranges and stone jars of home-made jam, even tea and coffee sent directly from Bewley's in Grafton Street, but which I knew came from her. From time to time I would send her a postcard, of St Finbarre's Cathedral or the holy shrine at Gougane Barra. I always wrote the same words: 'Love you, Mathilde. My heart and my stomach send their thanks and best wishes. Imogen.'

Father came down before the house was handed over to its new owners and together we cleared out the furniture and china. Some he took back to Lansdowne Road, mainly pictures, old photographs, family silver; most of the furniture went to a local auctioneer, except the things that I might want in my flat.

'I would like to see you comfortable,' he said, one afternoon, as we wrapped china in newspaper then laid it carefully into a series of tea chests. 'I would like to think that these pieces went towards making you comfortable. They have done that for so many people for so many years and now there is only you left.' He put a bundle into the chest and wandered over to the window. He looked down towards the sea, his face pale and melancholic. 'I used to think that we were such a family of energy and spirit. That was what it felt like when I was a child, but then it . . . We all disintegrated, disappeared, uncles, cousins, so many fled.'

He turned and looked at me. 'Why did they think they had to flee? What did they think they had done wrong?'

I, of course, couldn't answer that question.

'I could never go,' he said. 'And I had hoped that maybe . . .' He paused for a long while. 'I had hoped that Johnny would win an Olympic medal. That would have been something. Something.' He opened the window and stepped out into the garden and began to walk down the hill towards the jetty.

I wondered what to do. I wondered again about my invisibility. I wondered what I had done wrong; I echoed his thought. I dropped the piece of paper that I held in my hand on to the floor and stepped out through the window after him.

He walked fast, leaving a little trail behind him of bent and broken grass. I walked behind him; I didn't call out. I walked in his trail. The grass was wet and the promise of a frost hung in the air. He walked to the end of the jetty and stood looking out across the bay. I stood beside him. The water plocked and sighed beneath us.

After a long time he spoke.

'They say it was the energetic, the lively-minded who went, leaving the second-rate, the dismal behind, and the bigots, the political hacks, the self-servers. I never saw it like that. I only wanted to do a decent job in the place where I knew I was at home.'

He turned and looked at me. 'Will you also go?'

I laughed. 'Why should I do that?'

'We've buggered up your life, haven't we?'

'I'll survive. Here. Don't worry about me, Father.'

'I really don't know what happened. I suppose I have been like an ostrich keeping my head in the sand and then suddenly everything disintegrates. Humpty Dumpty falls off the wall.'

I said nothing. I didn't know how much he knew. I didn't want to make matters worse.

'Your great-uncle Harry was a champion swimmer too. Did I ever tell you that before?'

'No.'

'I don't think I told Johnny either. Not, I suppose, that it would have made any difference. What do you think?'

'Probably not.'

'I suppose I wanted too much from Johnny.'

'I think he thought so.'

'I never told him why. I think it was because of all those

[123]

people who had felt they had to go. I have left it too late to speak.'

'I don't suppose it would have made any difference. We don't think like that any more. Father . . .' I wanted to say to him that he was not to blame, that Johnny's disappearance had nothing to do with him. 'He loves you,' I said instead.

'I had left him the house in Dublin, in the interests of continuity. And you this place, of course. Fairity . . . But now . . .'

'That's all right, Father. Don't brood on it.'

'Now. How can I not brood, child?'

'I have no answer to that.'

'I suppose I shouldn't address you as "child"?'

'I'd rather you didn't.'

'You will always be "child" inside my head. He would have been, too. I sometimes think you take things like that too seriously. After all,' he gave a little laugh, 'you call me Father.'

It was the most personal conversation that we had ever had.

It was starting to get cold. He took a step towards the edge of the jetty, and for a moment I thought he was going to fall into the water.

'Johnny,' he shouted.

I nearly jumped out of my skin.

Onny . . . on . . . onnnny.

'Harry.'

Arry . . . ar . . . rry . . . ry.

'He swam from here too. All those . . .'

ry . . . ry . . .

'. . . years ago. My father used to tell me about him from time to time. He missed him. He used to come down here and call his name. Because he missed him. I caught him doing it once. I should have been asleep, but I was lying in bed with the window open and the full moon on my face and I heard this voice call out, "Harry". I didn't recognize the voice, it sounded so weird. I jumped out of bed and went to the window. "Harry", the voice called again, and then the echo answered and answered, and I thought, Who is this? What is this? And the name came back and back across the bay and then my father came up the field and I knew that it was he who had called out. I must have been about six. I had never before heard of Harry.' He turned and looked at me. 'You're cold. So am I. Let's go. Goodbye.'

He threw the word with all his power across the water, and as we moved away, the answer splintered around us, and hung in the bare branches of the trees.

Oooaye.

oo . . . oo . . . aa . . . ye.

aaye.

✳ ✳ ✳

I remember well the day we arrived back from Paradise at the end of the summer holidays to find the piano in the drawing room. The children must have been in the secret as they made some excuse to call me into the drawing room when I should have been attending to the unpacking and the resettling of the little ones into the nursery. I have to admit that I was in a little fuss when I entered the room, annoyed at having been, as I thought, unnecessarily disturbed.

There it was, the most beautiful Broadwood baby grand, with its own neat, cushioned stool sitting slantwise to the window in the back drawing room, the sun at that moment obligingly shining on the keys. Patrick stood, one hand resting on the polished lid, with an anxious smile on his face. The children stood in their stepping-stone heights beside him.

I noticed before I even saw the piano that Arthur was now taller than his father.

'Surprise,' shouted Millie, and then they all clapped.

'The most wonderful surprise in my whole life.'

I went across the room and touched it, just to

*make sure that it was real. I ran my hands over its
smoothness. I lifted the lid and propped it up, I
touched the strings and traced the golden letters
'Broadwood' with a finger.*

'It is real,' said Patrick.

'I don't know what to say. I may cry.'

*'Don't do that, woman, or I'll bring it back to the
shop. Why don't you try it?'*

'Yes, play. Please play, Mama,' said Rosie.

*I sat down and massaged my fingers: after two
months in Paradise they would be stiff, inflexible, and
I wanted to play with bravura, not like some
bumbling, fumbling, all-thumbs tub-thumper. I
stretched my fingers out wide and the sun shone over
my shoulder, just as it should, on to the keys and my
fingers, and I began to play.*

*' "See me dance the polka",' I sang. ' "See me leave
the ground. See my petticoats flying as my partner
whirls me round".'*

*Patrick held out his hand to Rosie and whirled
around the room with her, and the other children
began to dance too.*

*'One, two, three. Hop.' I heard Harry say to little
Maud. 'Hop, you muggins. H-O-P.'*

*The music turned into a reel and they continued to
dance, and I looked up from the keys and saw that the*

*two long windows that gave on to the street were open
and I liked the thought of our gaiety spilling out into
the street and perhaps making the passers-by smile too.*

*We all calmed down in time and I thanked Patrick
with proper words and a kiss or two.*

*When the children had gone and I sat at the piano,
my fingers dreaming on the keys, he came over to me.
'Have you forgiven me?'*

I stopped playing.

*The week before we had gone to Paradise he
had imposed his authority on me and I had reacted
in a somewhat undutiful way. I find the absoluteness
of male authority sometimes hard to bear. I do have
to say that Patrick has almost always been a fair
and liberal husband, even though he finds it very
hard to take on board some of the more modern
thinking that I am glad to say is having quite an
effect on the way in which people have to live. I have
insisted, and he has agreed with a certain good
humour, that the girls go to Alexandra School where
they receive an education that will fit them for
an independent life, if they should choose to lead
one. However, he has drawn the line at suffragism
among women and when I told him that I was going
to join the Women's Franchise League he put his foot
down. I might almost say that he stamped his foot. I*

had not the strength of will to defy him. I do hope that my daughters, when faced with such decisions as they undoubtedly will be, will have more confidence and courage than I have. Anyway, at that moment I looked past him along Upper Mount Street at the charming silhouette of the Pepper Canister Church. 'You have given me so much reason to be happy that I could go on thanking you for ever.'

'You haven't answered my question.'

'I think you shouldn't have asked it. You make me feel that you are buying my affection and loyalty. You shouldn't have to do that. I love you in spite of our differences and I hope you feel the same about me.'

He picked up my hand and kissed it. 'Darling Louisa, how lucky I am.'

'How lucky we both are.'

I don't suppose either of us thought then how sorrow could destroy our lives. I long to sleep and he to be awake, alive, filled with energy. He wishes me to be the same, but this time I can't any longer obey him: my will to be a dutiful wife has faded with my will to be alive.

There is one more song I wish to set to music and sing aloud and then I may have to go.

My third song for Harry.

The bumpy rhythm of the poem is beginning to assemble itself in my head.

> *A blackbird singing*
> *On a moss-upholstered stone,*
> *Bluebells swinging,*
> *Shadows wildly blown,*
> *A song in the wood,*
> *A ship on the sea.*
> *The song was for you*
> *And the ship was for me.*
>
> *A blackbird singing*
> *I hear in my troubled mind,*
> *Bluebells swinging*
> *I see in a distant wind.*
> *But sorrow and silence*
> *Are the wood's threnody,*
> *The silence for you*
> *And the sorrow for me.*

Chords and discords, a running, gasping air, rhythms and counter-rhythms all plait and unplait in my mind.

I will write the notes on the staves in my head: quavers, crotchets, minims, semi-quavers, my

*alphabet. The melody will take its own time to
gestate. I will sing it aloud, once or perhaps twice
when the house is empty, and then maybe I will be too
tired to go on living.*

* * *

It was pathetic, I thought, during my weeks of silence, that
they should have all scattered the way they did. Brothers,
sisters, cousins, over three generations, leaving me with no
one once Johnny was gone. So far and so fast they went, as
if they only lived to shake the dust of this country from
their heels. It was almost as if my great-grandmother's
death had given them leave to go. I don't suppose she had
that in mind. She hated the past and the present so much
that she never gave a thought to the future.

I like this dust.

Even during my weeks of silence I never contem-
plated the idea of running away or dying, or hiding myself
totally in madness. I had only wanted to keep my secret
in my head, imprisoned there for as long as was necessary,
and the only possible way to do this was to remain
dumb.

Keep mum.

Lips buttoned.

Total silence.

Mind you, it never occurred to me that that would have me locked up.

Mathilde had the right idea. 'She's just giving her tongue a rest,' she said to Sylvia, on day three of my silence. 'And no harm. There's no harm in silence.' She had laid her hand on my head, warm and gentle, and I could smell cinnamon from her and I nearly spoke. I nearly said the one word 'cinnamon'. The word reached the tip of my tongue and then wouldn't move any further, so maybe I was mad after all. I thought I had my voice under control, but perhaps I was wrong.

'You don't know anything about it, Mathilde,' said Sylvia.

'I know about a lot,' said Mathilde.

'Well, go, just go now. I want to speak to the child alone.' My mother's voice was rough.

I looked towards Mathilde to see how she had taken the roughness of tone. She nodded and stood up.

When she was in the house, and except to go to Mass she seldom left it, she wore green felt slippers embroidered with cheerful flowers. She walked silently in her lovely slippers to the door and left the room.

Sylvia sat down beside me in the chair that Mathilde had been in. 'Imogen,' she said.

I, of course, said nothing.

She took my hand and stroked my fingers with her

thumb. 'Look, I don't know what all this is about, but we can't sort it out until you talk to us.'

There was a long silence and I wondered if Mathilde was listening at the door. I was sitting up in my bed, supported by a large number of soft pillows.

'Can we?' she asked.

I gestured with my hands. 'I cannot speak', the gesture was meant to mean. If I could speak we wouldn't have a problem.

'We believe, your father and I and, of course, Dr Salmon, that you are having some sort of nervous break-down. This sort of thing happens from time to time with girls your age. There is no finality about it. It will pass. You will be restored to your ... equilibrium. Yes. There is no doubt about that. You don't need to worry about that.'

I wasn't. I moved my head fretfully on my pillows and closed my eyes, an indication, I hoped, of drowsiness. It had no effect.

'It is what to do now. Before things maybe get worse. We could just wait and see how everything develops, but we think, your father and I, that a short spell in a nursing-home would be the best thing.'

I opened my eyes and stared at her. I waited.

She picked up a pad and a pen from the table by my bed and offered them to me. 'Write,' she said. She took my right hand and pressed the fingers round the pen. 'Write.'

I shook my head.

She sighed. 'I will leave the paper by you and if you feel you have anything ... anything at all that you should communicate to us, please write it down. I do not believe that you have lost the ability to write. We want to help you, Imogen. Believe that. We love you. We have your best interests at heart.' She stood up and bent down as if to kiss me, but I turned my head away.

You see, you must see, that I deserved what I got: I was as unfeeling, unforgiving, unbalanced as the rest, except perhaps Father, who I believe moved in some dreamlike world of his own. I have seen so many like him, men who, in appearance, attend to their own work, their families, but in reality live in another world of defeated dreams and longings. Men who have lost, for some reason, the energy of their fathers and hope that in their sons they may regain it once more.

If Johnny had allowed himself to become a swimming hero my father would have basked most happily in the reflected glory. Of course, at that time, when I was seventeen and about to be put away in some sort of madhouse, I had no such thoughts in my head. I thought that grown-up people were whole people and the process of growing up was the process of finding that wholeness.

* * *

In my father's diary for 1970 I read the following:

A cold and unfriendly February day. We drove to
Newtownmountkennedy through sheeting rain to
bring Imogen to the nursing-home. I believe we
have made the right decision.

Yes, I do. Yes.

The child has become completely withdrawn
from us and from a normal way of living. I have
had to rely on Sylvia's wisdom in this matter. I am
merely a knitter together of broken bones and
know little or nothing of broken minds. The
shrinkman, chosen by Sylvia, seems to think that a
complete separation from her home and the
therapy of total calmness and a few well-chosen
drugs will have her right as rain in a short while. I
do hope he is correct. His reputation as someone
who can deal with the growing problems of the
young is high.

An early-Victorian house surrounded by a most
charming and kempt garden. We were greeted
with warmth and cups of tea, greatly appreciated
after our drive. Imogen's room is pleasant and
comfortable, the staff smile and smile and the

matron is . . . well, what can I say? A matron.
Imogen seemed unconcerned about whether we
stayed or left or indeed when we might see her
again: her eyes just gazed through us as if we
didn't exist. I suppose I would have liked her
to shed a tear as we left. When we arrived home I
shut myself in my room and listened to the
Missa Santa Cecelia of Scarlatti. This was a prayer
for my daughter. I hope it will be recognized as
such.

I made a note to go to Tower Records in Wicklow
Street and buy myself Scarlatti's Mass. I haven't got round
to it yet, but I will. I would like to know what sort of a
prayer my father offered up on my behalf. Maybe a spot of
Billie Holiday would have been more appropriate.

'Oooh, what a little moonlight can do.
Wait a while till a little moonbeam comes peeping through.'

* * *

Sometimes I used to cycle into town after school and
have tea with Johnny in his rooms in college. None of
them ever called the place Trinity or even TCD. It was
always 'college' they said when they spoke about the

place. I was glad to discover little things like that.

He shared three rooms and a scummy kitchen with a man from Athlone called Martin something-or-other. They weren't friends, just passing acquaintances, polite in the scummy kitchen and each keeping an eye out for a better option. I was sitting at the table in Johnny's room one day doing my homework when he put his head round the door. 'Hi,' he said. 'Johnno around?'

'He'll be back soon. He has a three o'clock lecture.'

'And you are?'

'Sister.'

'Do you have a name?'

'Imogen.'

He raised his eyebrows. 'Would you give the lad a message? I'm Martin. Just in case he's wondering, I'm away off home for the weekend. It's my sister's birthday. Can't miss that, don't you know? He probably won't notice I'm not here, but if he does, that's where I am. Back Sunday night. Ever been to Athlone?'

'No.'

'Lucky you. Tra-la.' He was gone, slamming the outside door and clattering down the stone stairs.

I got on with my work. I used to do this from time to time, invade uninvited his rooms, use uninvited his chair and table, spread myself in his space. I liked the feeling of being in a world of energetic people. The footsteps below the window, voices calling, laughter from time to time, doors banging. Home was so quiet now without Johnny, so carpeted and voiceless, each person shut in their own world, no trading of thoughts and dreams. My energies from now on would be focused on getting into college. I would work as Johnny had worked, this would be where I would disentangle the confusions in my head. I liked that notion. I liked at that moment, as I waited for Johnny to appear, the idea of clarity, of discovery.

It never occurred to me that little would be different: that the high grey walls, the classical buildings were merely another backdrop for the same old world. I heard his whistling first and then the door opened and he came in and threw his books along the passageway. He slouched into the room and saw me at the table. He did not look very pleased. 'What are you doing here?'

'I'm so pleased to see you too.'

'For God's sake, Im, don't be cute. I've had a bloody awful day. Wall-to-wall lectures. Now I'm going out for a drink. So . . .'

'Can I come too?'

'No. You get along home. Why do you have to come in here to do your homework anyway? You've got a perfectly good room of your own.'

I gathered my books together and shoved them into my shoulder-bag. He walked over to the window and looked down into the square.

'Sorry, Im,' he said. 'I just feel a bit fed up today. Sorry.'

'I just miss you round the place. I miss your ugly mug. I rather like working here. I can imagine I'm . . . I'm sorry too. I didn't think . . .'

'OK. That's OK. Just pop along now, there's a good girl. I'll be round sometime over the weekend. We'll make an arrangement to do something then. We might go to the flicks.'

I nodded. I headed for the door: no point in staying or arguing, or anything at all.

'Goodbye.'

' 'Bye, Im. Take care. See you, pet.'

I closed the door behind me and went down the stairs. Outside little stabs of sleet were in the air. I unlocked my bike and began to wheel it towards Front Square. A couple of young men passed me. They were laughing and possibly a little high.

'Oh, Johnny baby,' one of them called, as they reached his steps. 'Ooooh, Johnny baby baby baby.'

✳   ✳   ✳

One dusky evening, pedalling along Shelbourne Road, on

my way back from school, my head down and legs pushing hard against the wind and swirling rain – how I have always hated February – a car honked and stopped by the kerb on the other side of the road. Bruno rolled down the window and leaned out. He beckoned me over. A passing car splashed me wickedly with muddy water.

I pushed my bike across the road. 'Hello, what are you doing here?'

'I have been at your house. I called to see you. I had an hour to spare and I wanted to see you.'

'I have school, you idiot.'

'I get mixed up with the times.'

'I never get home before half past four. What a shame. Come back with me now and have a cup of tea.'

He shook his head. 'I cannot, *liebchen*. I have to be back by five. I am on duty. I am almost late. I stayed as long as I could. I will not be so foolish another time.'

He looked wonderful, shining with happiness. He was, of course, also dry and warm tucked neatly inside his car.

'Give me a cold wintry kiss,' he said. 'I will give you a little bit of warmth and then you can remember me until Saturday when I intend to take you to the pictures. Johnny and I intend to take you. He insists on coming. I say to him, "No, Johnny, two is company," but he just laughs. He has no sense of propriety, your brother.'

I put my head in the window and he kissed me. His mouth was warm and soft. I felt disadvantaged and tears jumped all of a sudden into my eyes. No further. They quivered there and he banged me on the nose with a finger. 'Home you go and get dry. Mathilde will scold you when she comes in if she sees you like this.'

He drove off. I stood by the side of the road and watched the car until it reached the junction with Ballsbridge. The indicator light flashed and the car turned right towards the heart of town. I longed to be grown-up, to move among college people with confidence, to know all the secrets that they knew, to wear red nail polish and colour my hair as the mood took me and, above all at that moment, to understand about love.

✳ ✳ ✳

17 March

Snow.

The day of our glorious Welsh patron saint.

I left the house early and slithered along the County Wicklow roads to visit Imogen. It has been a couple of weeks since I saw the child, though I have telephoned every second day to find out about her progress.

Sylvia has not been down to the clinic (as she

calls it) at all and said to me only yesterday when I asked her to come with me on my visit. 'The child needs a holiday from her family. You go by all means, if you wish. Yes, you must do as you wish.'

It wasn't real snow, just the occasional flurry of flakes that didn't lie on the road but added to the discomfort of driving. I drove across Bray Head and wondered as I drove if maybe Sylvia was right and I should leave the child alone. I cannot believe this to be the right thing to do. I remember my father telling me about his own mother's withdrawal from the gregarious life of the family, little by little until she seemed to be merely a ghost in the house, resting behind closed doors or playing the piano to herself, strange unrecognizable pieces according to Father. Towards the end of her life, he told me, if you went into the drawing room when she was playing, she would close down the lid of the piano and sit, hands folded in her lap, smiling but unspeaking. Is this what lies in front of Imogen? Are we all condemned to be infected by our past?

I pulled the car in by the railway bridge just beyond Greystones and walked under it on to the beach. I was surprised by how calm the sea was, grey as far as the eye could see, no sign of horizon,

just greyness and the occasional grey gull coasting
on the wind. It was too cold to stay long: the east
wind battered my face and sang above me in the
telegraph wires. I walked head down for about a
hundred yards and then, before turning back, I
shouted up to the clouds, 'Hail, glorious St
Patrick,' just to let the Welsh rogue know that I
too, in my own way, was prepared to acknowledge
his achievement in civilising the weird beings who
were our ancestors and, of course, in dispersing the
snakes.

Nothing, of course, was solved in my head by
this cold hiatus in my journey. Imogen was in her
room, standing by the window and looking down
into the garden. Daffodils were just starting to
show yellow in swathes under the trees. I
commented on this and she smiled. I also told her
how cold it was and how the snow had blown in
flurries as I drove from the city and the east wind
had stung my bare face on Greystones beach. She
appeared to be listening and when I stopped
talking she put out a hand and touched my cheek.
She looked pale and her hair hung down over her
shoulders like a shining veil, but she smiled. I
think this must be a good sign. I wish I knew more
about disorders of the mind.

The nurse who was sitting at a small table in the corner of the room writing something in a notebook said suddenly into the silence, 'We brushed her hair a hundred times this morning. Didn't we, Imogen? Don't you think it looks pretty?'

'Yes.'

'I washed it last night and dried it with a little hair-dryer that Matron lent us. She has such pretty hair.'

'Yes,' I said again.

'She's looking more herself, don't you think?'

'Yes.'

'When the weather gets a little warmer she'll be able to take a little run in the garden. That will put some colour in her cheeks.'

'Yes.'

The nurse looked expectantly at me. She had done her bit, her face said, now it was up to me. I couldn't think of anything to say. I bowed politely towards her. 'I must be on my way . . .'

'So soon? I could bring you a cup of coffee.' She turned to Imogen. 'You'd like Daddy to stay and have a cup of coffee, wouldn't you, dear?'

Imogen glanced at me with a slight smile on her face. Slowly she shook her head and then turned back to stare at the garden.

'I think I must go,' I said to the nurse. 'The roads are awful. I said I'd be home in time for ...'

I stopped. What was the point? I touched my daughter's long, shining hair. 'Soon,' was all I said to her. 'Soon.' I nodded to the nurse. 'Goodbye.'

'Goodbye, Doctor. Matron's away off up to Dublin to see the parade. Otherwise ...'

'No ... I ... That's all right. Goodbye. Thank you. Goodbye.'

The child never moved.

I looked back at the house before I got into the car. A figure stood at her window, quite still. I raised my hand and waved.

* * *

I remember that day.

I remember because of the hair-washing.

Nurse was kind.

I sat on a chair and leaned my head backwards over the basin and the shampoo smelt sweet, like fruit, and then she poured jug after jug of warm water over my head to rinse out the suds, and she chattered as she rubbed and smoothed at my hair. I don't remember what she talked about, just the sound of her voice up and down mixed in with the splashing from the taps and the jugs of warm water cascading over my head and her firm fingers squeezing and wringing until she was satisfied that there was no soap left, and she wrapped a huge towel round my head and rubbed until my head ached.

I also remember one other thing that he has not mentioned: he had brought me a bunch of shamrock. I held it in my hand as I looked out of the window at the daffodils and this man who waved and then drove away. I turned from the window and found that Nurse had gone from the room, no doubt to report to some higher authority about the non-event of my father's visit, I poured some water into my tooth-glass, placed the shamrock in it and put it beside my bed. Then I sat on the bed and cried. That was the moment when I realized that I would have to speak again.

Speak, and at the same time keep silent.

* * *

Little Edward thrives.

Helen brings him round to see me on Thursday afternoons, Nanny's afternoon off, I presume. I watch her pushing the perambulator along Upper Mount Street and I pack away all my private thoughts and prepare to smile for half an hour or so, until she takes

the little fellow away again. It is kind of her to be so
thoughtful. She and Arthur are occupied with all the
details of buying a house in Lansdowne Road and
decorating it and she brings with her scraps of
wallpaper and curtain material, velvets, linens,
chintzes for chairs and sofas. She chatters energetically
and I watch the little fellow crawl on the carpet and
perform the charming tricks that small children know
will always seduce grown-ups. I smile at Helen and
commend her taste and energy and finally I pick up
Edward and sit him on my knee at the piano and play
for him.

There was an old woman as I've heard tell
Fa la falalalala
And she went to market her eggs for to sell.
Fa la falalalala.

He likes that one and claps his hands.
That was Harry's favourite.

There was a man lived in the moon, lived in the moon,
lived in the moon.
There was a man lived in the moon,
And his name was Aiken Drum.
And he played upon a ladle, a ladle, a ladle,

He played upon a ladle,
And his name was Aiken Drum.

He stretches out his fat little fingers and grasps at the notes, as Harry used to do, and laughs a little chuckling well-remembered laugh and I have to call out to Helen. 'Go. Now you must go. You are such lovely people and now I must rest.'

I watch her wheel the baby back along Upper Mount Street again until at the church she turns right and is out of my view. In spite of the peace, life is still edgy here, and the thought of any harm coming to Helen and the child makes my hands tremble with fear.

Tomorrow they go down to Paradise, Patrick, Arthur and his little family, and Millie, who spends most of her time down there, these days, and I will be alone here for two weeks. 'Alone' is, of course, an absurd word to use as the servants will be here as always to mind me and make sure that I am safe and comfortable. I think that Patrick believes that their presence in the house will prevent me from doing anything 'foolish'.

He is, of course, right.

The work on the third Ledwidge song is going in fits and starts; my initial energy has drained somewhat

and I now find I have to work very hard at addressing
the strange rhythms in the first four lines of each verse.
I write and erase all on the staves in my mind. I play
and am silent for perhaps two or three hours at a time.

A ship on the sea.

Those simple words
I cannot fit to music.

The song was for you, and the ship was for me.

I cannot fit to music.
When I think of ships all I can see are those vessels
filled with young men heading through the
Mediterranean to Turkey. I want a lament, with an
element of the traditional in it, but only an element.
There is a wandering thread of melody in my head but
I find it hard to capture. Maybe this time I will have
to use pen and paper, but the thought of that frightens
me. I want my music to die with me.

✳ ✳ ✳

This all seems very one-sided. I have written nothing
at all about our mother's family. This is because I know little

about it. She had been born in England, the only child of an Irish father who had gone to live near Amersham just after the First World War. My grandfather had served in the RAMC and, as far as I can gather, had no desire to return to the possibility of another war, more violence, and an uncertain future, so he opted for the safety of the English Home Counties. He married a local girl, who died giving birth to my mother, and apart from that tragedy he lived in safety as a GP until 1945 when he was killed by a flying bomb while on a visit to London.

These are bare enough bones, I know.

I have often wondered where he was when he died.

They always used to say that as long as you heard the noise of the bomb in the air you were safe. It was the silence that was dangerous.

I wonder where he was when he heard that silence, and then did he for a moment wish that he had stayed at home in Ireland? Was that his last thought?

Perhaps he had no time for a last thought.

My mother was not the sort of person to whom you could address such questions.

I have always wondered why I wanted to ask such questions. Other people seem to get on very well without being nosy . . . That was what Mathilde used to call me.

'Miss Nosy. Why do you ask such things, Miss Nosy?'

'Because I want to know.'

'And maybe I don't want to tell you. Maybe knowing too much is bad for little girls.'

'But how do you learn, Mathilde, if you can't ask questions?'

'If you are too sharp, you cut yourself.'

When she said things like that to me, I used to laugh, only for a moment or two, and then I would go back to my questions.

'Are Jews bad?'

'Such a question. Not bad, not good, just like all other people.'

'If they're not bad why did you stop being a Jew?'

'I want to live happily for ever in Ireland, so I think to myself, Better be a Catholic, Mathilde. That is the best thing to be. So I take instructions.'

'What are instructions?'

'They were classes, teaching me how to be a good Catholic.'

'Are you a good Catholic?'

'I am a good Catholic, with my own secrets.'

'Are you allowed to have secrets?'

'I don't know, child. Now, will you please stop this interrogation? Everyone has secrets.'

'I bet Sylvia and Daddy don't have secrets.'

She said nothing.

'Mathilde?'

She sighed. 'More questions? Only one more I answer, and then you must go and do your homework.'

'Did the Jews really kill Jesus Christ?'

'You will break my heart. Circumstances, politics, happenings killed him. Not just Jews.'

'Like the Irish killed Micheal Collins?'

'You could say that, but I don't think people would like you to say it.'

'Why don't you become a Jew again?'

Her eyes filled with tears and I realised that I had gone on too long with my questions. I was sorry, but I was not satisfied. There were so many things I wanted to know. She didn't cry. She just looked into the fire for a moment or two.

'I am too tired,' she said, at last.

* * *

That winter of 1970, as well as the icy wind and swirling snow showers, we had a long, hard frost: icicles hung from the eaves, and the railway signals in Lansdowne Road froze up and no trains ran for several days. Nothing belonging to nature had any colour: clouds, sea, earth, trees were all grey and black and a pale sad brown like old, old photographs in family albums. Even the birds, cats and dogs seemed drab. Each morning for about two weeks mist pressed against the windows, like a grey curtain. It would disappear during the course of the day and return as night fell.

One Saturday morning I went down late for breakfast and found Bruno standing in the hall. 'Lazybones,' he said.

'What are you doing here?'

'Looking for you. If you eat up your breakfast quickly we will go and get Johnny and go to skate in the Phoenix Park.'

'Skate? I can't skate. I have never skated.'

'It's time you learn.'

'I have no skates.'

'Leave all these details to me. Go and have your breakfast. Don't be too long or all the world will be there before us.' He went into the drawing room and I heard him talking to Sylvia.

If you were late for breakfast you had to eat it in the kitchen. Mathilde was stacking plates in the dishwasher.

'I'm going skating.'

She raised her eyebrows.

I was crunching my way through a bowl of cornflakes before she spoke: 'You'll probably break an ankle.'

'I can't think why you say a thing like that.'

'A lot of people break an ankle when they skate, or a wrist. It is easy also to break a wrist. When you fall you put out a hand like this.' She put out her right hand as if to save herself. 'And snap!'

I laughed. 'I won't do that. I'll cling to Bruno like grim death.'

'Don't lean backwards. Always just a little forward, not, of course, so that you look all hunched up, just a little balancing forwards.' She closed the dishwasher door with a snap. 'When I was your age I was the best of skaters. I know what I am talking about. Lean forward. Wrap up well. It will be cold for you in your learning state.' She left the room.

Sylvia was standing with Bruno in the hall when I went upstairs. He dangled a pair of skating boots in his hand. 'Look. I told you I would find boots for you and I find them under your very nose. Sylvia had them hidden away.'

'Don't lose them,' my mother murmured. 'I might need them myself some day.'

'How could I lose them?'

'You,' she said meanly, 'could lose anything.' She turned to Bruno and gave him one of her wonderful smiles. 'Do make sure she doesn't break any bones.'

Mathilde was right: it was cold.

I wobbled with Bruno.

I wobbled with Johnny, who had cottoned on to the notion rather more quickly than I seemed to be able to do.

I wobbled between the two of them then retired to the

edge of the lake to rest my aching ankles. After a few minutes Johnny joined me and we sat and watched Bruno swooping and gliding and twirling, backwards and forwards, the ice sighing and crackling and at times singing beneath him. The other skaters stopped and watched him too, and clapped as he performed each brilliant movement.

'Talk about showing off,' said Johnny.

'I think he's wonderful.'

Johnny put an arm around my shoulder. 'So do I,' he whispered.

We sat there hugging together against the cold; I could feel my heart jolting inside me each time he passed close to us and smiled, and I think I could feel Johnny's heart doing the same thing. Finally the exhibition came to an end with a series of spinning turns, up and down like a child's top, little sparks of ice flying out from under his skates, his face polished by the wind.

'Bravo,' someone shouted, and there was a scattering of applause. Johnny took his arm from my shoulders and I bent down and began to unlace my mother's boots, but my fingers were cold and I fumbled unsuccessfully at the double knot.

'Why don't you come and have a twirl with me?'

I looked up. He was standing beside me, looking like a hero.

I shook my head. 'No, thanks.'

He held his hand out to Johnny, who took it, and they both twirled away from me arm in arm, hands locked together, hip and thigh touching hip and thigh. Bruno said something into Johnny's ear and Johnny laughed. I struggled with the knot and the sun that had been shining was covered by grey clouds.

* * *

I was afraid that when I began to speak again they would interrogate me.

Please try to remember.

Please try to tell us.

It will be for your own good in the end.

Please.

Always polite.

They would always be polite, I knew that.

They would take notes.

They would smile.

Imogen, Imogen, please, we are here to help you, they would say with sincerity in their voices.

They will feel so happy that I have found my voice again.

They will feel proud that they have caused such a tentative recovery.

Will they make me drop my guard with their kindness?

Will they give me lulling drinks or perhaps the insidious needle?

Such notions frighten me, not because maybe I will tell them the things I don't want ever to speak about, but that such drugs dripped into the body can lurk for years, can bend and distort the delicate membranes of the mind for ever. I can't, though, remain for ever mute, so I will take it gently.

Take them gently, I said to myself inside my head.

I let such thoughts and questions run through my mind for several days. I practised speaking aloud to myself alone at night under the bedclothes. I would whisper and murmur short words, my hands folded across my mouth in case I spoke too loud and some passing nurse in the passageway might hear me.

Hallo.

Anyone there?

Yes.

I.

I, Imogen.

I am Imogen.

Alive.

Speaking.

Alive.

I will speak for ever. Yes.

And so on. So long ago now, and yet I remember well

the warmth of my bed and the warmth of my breath against my hands as I spoke.

Truth, I said once.

The word sounded good on my tongue and in my breath: a good, rich word, but I realised that I wasn't sure what it meant. It was a dangerous word.

I would have to use such a word with caution.

I could manage that all right.

I am.

Sane.

Secure now in my sanity.

I said that into my pillow with my fingers crossed for good luck.

I am.

Sane.

It was on a Tuesday that I spoke first.

I was lying in bed relishing the stretch in the morning light. A bright sunrise caused the shadows of the bars on the window to fall on the wall beside my bed, so for a while I seemed to be doubly imprisoned, but nevertheless light-hearted.

Nurse came in with my breakfast on a tray; I was still treated as an invalid as well as someone not quite right in the head. She was wearing blue and her early-morning cheery smile. 'Time to rise and shine,' she said. She put the tray down on the table beside my bed.

'Want to run along to the toilet before brek?'

I shook my head and sat up.

She rearranged the pillows behind me. 'There we go. Slept well? Healing. Sleep is healing. One of the most healing things. There is nothing like a long good night's sleep. Everyone will tell you that.'

I remembered something from school. ' "Knits up the ravel'd sleeve of care," ' I said.

She stopped fiddling with the pillows and looked at me. Blue eyes matched blue dress. 'Imogen . . .' she said.

'Shakespeare. "Macbeth".'

'Isn't that wonderful now? You've found your voice.'

I wanted to smile at her, but I began to cry instead. I wasn't exactly crying, just silent, unwanted tears rolling down my cheeks; relief, I think, rather than sorrow, was pumping them out.

'There,' said Nurse. 'There, there, there.'

She took my hand and held it in hers for a moment. Then she took a white handkerchief from her pocket and handed it to me. 'A hankie, dear,' she said. 'Young people nowadays never have hankies.'

As I wiped my face she poured a cup of tea. 'You have a good drink of this and I'll run and see Matron. She'll be so pleased. Will you be all right if I leave you for a few minutes?'

I nodded.

She left the room and I sat in bed with a white hand-kerchief in one hand and a cup of tea steaming gently in the other.

Recovery seemed to have set in.

✳ ✳ ✳

This morning I found an old music manuscript book in the bottom drawer of the escritoire in the back drawing room. Page after page of empty staves. I had been looking for a book of Chopin Nocturnes that I thought had been put in there some years ago, but found this instead and some old envelopes addressed to Patrick from Rugby School, presumably containing the boys' term reports and suchlike. I will take these out and read them in a day or so. I feel I must now get down to this piece of composition. I had thought that perhaps I might intertwine the sound of the voice with a melancholic echo, the bird aping almost the human voice, an ironic distortion, and then in the left hand the pulse of the sea. Something about this makes me think of the echo at Paradise and the pleasure the children have always found in their boisterous shouting across the bay. More cheerful, that, than my little song will be.

It will be curious to see my melodies written down.

I hope my imagination will not be inhibited by the process.

There has been a call on the telephone from Patrick to say that they all arrived safely at Paradise and that little Edward was none the worse for the long motor journey and is already thriving in the mild spring sunshine.

'And you, my darling, you are well, I hope, not allowing yourself to be too drawn down into melancholy.'

I am well, thank you, Patrick.

✳ ✳ ✳

I found no letters from the school in the trunk, but I did find a little velvet bag in which were four medals on faded striped ribbons. Each one had a date on the back, 1911, 1912, 1913 and 1914. Rugby School, Swimming, 1st Prize.

I polished them up and put them in the glass case that held my grandfather's war medals. This seemed the right thing to do, and I was sorry that no one had done it before me. I do believe in the importance of personal acts of courage, fortitude, honesty, skill, wartime or peacetime, domestic or public: the act that sets you apart from the crowd, no matter how trivial it may seem, should be treasured in memory.

I wish, like my father had wished, that Johnny had stuck with his swimming and tried for the Olympic squad: no matter what had happened to him after that, the very notion of that endeavour would have clung with him, perhaps warmed him on cold days.

I wish I had been able to find the manuscript book in which my great-grandmother had written her threnody. I would like to have been able to fumble with my fingers and my voice at her music. How astonishing it would be to discover a hidden talent or genius maybe, another woman stifling her creative energy in the interest of calm, equilibrious living. We keep digging them up all the time, these days. Maybe, of course, my great-grandmother was a woman of little talent, just turning out sentimental rubbish of little or no worth and best kept to herself. I like to be a bit romantic about this. I like the thought that in her secret struggle to create music were the seeds of my own more public success with words. I owe her that.

I acknowledge that.

I thank her.

Louisa.

I thank.

I . . . ank . . . annnnk.

✳ ✳ ✳

We received a phone call this morning from the nursing-home, just as I was about to leave for my surgery, to say that Imogen had found her voice. That was not the way they put it, merely my untechnical way of writing it down. Owing to pressure of work I will not be able to get down to see her until the weekend, but I hope Sylvia will be able to find the time to make the journey. I suspect she will not. I also suspect that she has neither the inclination for the longish drive nor the warmth of feeling for the child that would make her anxious to go. Perhaps this is for the best: maybe at this moment Imogen is too fragile to take a meeting with either of her parents. It would be tragic if her voice were to disappear again.

I only spoke briefly to Dr McGuinness. 'First step. First step,' he said.

'I know nothing about the brain,' I said to him, and then I laughed a little nervously.

'And I, dear chap, know nothing about orthopaedic surgery. Let's just leave it like that. I won't expect you to tell me your secrets and you won't expect me to tell me mine.'

I hate people who call me 'my dear chap'. But let that pass. They say he is good at his job.

[163]

I wonder where we have gone wrong.

I wonder how many parents say that to each other every day.

I never felt anything other than an unturbulent affection for my parents and of course my Aunt Millie. She frightened me a little bit only because she saw no reason to behave like other people did; she would arrive on our doorstep here unannounced and disappear again when the notion took her, equally unannounced.

She once gave me a ferret, golden sleek and friendly, but with a rather pungent smell. Aunt Millie took it from the capacious pocket of her raincoat and handed it to me. 'This is for you, boy.'

My mother screamed. Aunt Millie took the animal from my hands gently.

I was sent to wash and by the time I came back both Millie and the golden animal were gone.

She always called me 'boy'. I suppose it saved her the trouble of trying to remember my name. I know my mother thought she was mad, but I never did and I don't think my father did either, just a woman who was privileged enough to be able to spend her life exactly as she wished.

My grandmother, on the other hand, was considered to be mad by everyone. For the last few

years of her life she is said to have wished for no
company but her own. According to my mother,
she would spend all her days shut in the drawing
room in Lower Fitzwilliam Street playing strange
tunes on the piano and sometimes singing, always
becoming thinner and paler, her eyes sinking
deeper and deeper into her head, until one night
she left the house when everyone was asleep and
walked up the hill, along Fitzwilliam Square,
striding out, I feel, her mind full of purpose,
crossing Leeson Street to the canal. Silent streets,
the gas lamps and the tall houses stretched away
behind her down towards the centre of the city, as
she walked, and in front of her the rim of distant
hills, the dark sky and stars, I have always hoped
that there were stars, and she slipped from the lock
gates into the canal and was found the next day,
like Ophelia, caught in weeds and dead branches,
her body half on the bank and half in the water. I
have not discussed this with Dr McGuinness. I do
not believe that my grandmother's madness has
anything to do with him. I don't think that I have
ever told Sylvia this story either. I never saw any
reason to. She has always been the sort of person to
scoff at weakness.

I hate the thought that Imogen may be

condemned to intermittent madness because of some weakness in my genes.

Was Johnny's death an act of madness or was it desperation of some sort?

Or me.

Am I mad?

I have had such longings in me down all the years that I have not dared to face, that even now I cannot write down.

I remember the disgust and contempt in my father's voice when he told me about Harry, and the sickening feeling that came to me that my father believed that had Harry been, as my father called it, 'normal' he would not have died at Suvla Bay.

Death was his punishment.

I wanted so much to laugh at such a Godforsaken notion, but I kept silent instead.

Like Imogen?

Perhaps like Imogen.

✳ ✳ ✳

I asked for books. It seemed to be the sensible thing to do.

After Matron and the doctor and various people had been to see me, had congratulated me and confabulated with me and asked me quite cautious questions to begin with, I asked for books.

I was tired of talking by then, and they were obviously alarmed by the thought that I might retreat into silence again. I think I could have winkled anything I wanted from them at that moment. I smiled to show them that I had no intention of being anything other than helpful: they were not to know that I would tell them nothing.

I wanted to read, either propped up by big soft pillows in bed, or in the armchair by the window, so that when I paused to turn my thoughts on what I had just read, I could look down on the garden and see the winter creeping away and the gardener raking the beds and removing the detritus of the stormy season.

It never occurred to me at that time that I might be happy to go home. I had to build up my confidence and energy to do that. Books, it seemed to me, were where I would find strength.

I made a list for them to relay to my father. I knew that there would be nothing nourishing on the shelves of the home.

'War and Peace'. 'Ulysses'. '*À la recherche du temps perdu*'.

Stop right there, I said to myself. Whatever happened to small and beautiful? '*L'Étranger*'. '*Symphonie Pastorale*'. Both in English, please.

Edna O'Brien, John McGahern, the writers who were scandalising the protectors of our morals. 'The Tailor and Anstey.' I remembered hearing about the book being ritually burnt and the author being held up to public shame.

Yes. I would like to read all the burnt books of the world . . . but then maybe I would not be in here, in my comfortable prison, for long enough. I tore up my list and put the pieces into the wastepaper basket.

'No, I don't remember anything. Nothing.'

'I just couldn't speak. I woke up and my tongue was like lead. I couldn't move it. Neither up nor down. Leaden. I woke up and my tongue was like lead. I couldn't move it. Neither up nor down. Leaden.'

'No. My fingers wouldn't hold a pen.'

'I don't know.'

'I have forgotten.'

'My mind is blank.'

'I feel well now. A bit tired.'

'I can speak, but I cannot remember.'

'Anything. I cannot.'

'Why do I have to say the same thing over and over again? Reiterate?'

'No. I have nothing to hide. No trauma, sorrow, fear. No, I have never wanted to kill myself. I am only just beginning. Why end it so soon? I can't see why.'

'No. I have no recollection.'

'Exams.'

'I have never enjoyed exams, but I did understand the need for them.'

'No, I have not been working too hard. Just drifting. That is all I have ever done. Drift. I enjoy that.'

'No. It is all I have to say. No. I do not remember.'

'Thank you. May I go now? I find these interrogations quite tiring. I would like to sleep for a while and then read.'

Spring came in through the open, though of course barred, windows and caressed my face with its warm fingers.

The nurse wore green or blue or pale pink, and very occasionally navy blue, but always the white shoes.

Father and, surprisingly, Sylvia came to see me.

It was a beautiful afternoon.

Father carried a box of books, which he put down on the floor of my room with a little puff of breath. 'I chose them myself,' he said. 'I wasn't sure . . .'

'Thanks. I'm sure they'll be great. Thanks.' I would have been happy to devour 'Noddy in Toyland' at that moment. 'Hello, Sylvia. Thanks for coming.'

She smiled. She touched my shoulder with a hand. She looked around the room as if she had never seen it before. Maybe she hadn't. There really were some things that I couldn't remember. 'Matron said we could take you for a drive.'

'If you liked,' said Father.

'It's such a lovely day.'

'Could we go to a beach?'

'Or up into the mountains.'

'I'd rather go to a beach.'

'Whatever you like,' said my father.

'Glendalough.'

'I'd rather go to a beach.'

Sylvia sighed. She looked very pale. 'Through the Wicklow Gap to Blessington.'

'I think we'll go to Greystones beach,' said my father. 'We don't want to tire her out.'

We walked along the passage and down the stairs, one of them on each side of me, like warders. 'How's Johnny?' I asked.

'We don't see very much of him.'

They each took one of my arms as we walked across the gravel to the car. I looked up at the house and saw the matron standing in the window of her office, watching us.

At the car Sylvia spoke. 'They say you don't remember anything.'

'That's right. Nothing.'

'I should try hard, if I were you. They could keep you here for ages. They're only trying to help, you know. One has to know the reason.'

My father opened the door and she slid into the front seat. 'I thought Imogen should sit in front.'

Sylvia smiled at us both. 'She doesn't mind. Do you, darling?'

I got into the back. 'I can't remember what I've forgotten,' I said. 'Stands to reason.'

* * *

I passed this morning in my room.

I had Teresa come and brush my hair. Five hundred long strokes.

The sun shone outside, but a cold east wind blew dust and papers up the street and people had to hold on to their hats.

I like having my hair brushed, although it is a pleasure in which I seldom indulge. Teresa has better things to do with her time. My hair is straight and fine and as she brushes it flies out around my head and little sparks and crackles run between the brush and the strands caused by the cold dryness of the air. This makes me feel light-headed and makes Teresa smile.

So many years ago Patrick used to brush my hair at night and run his hands through its golden silkiness and kiss it and kiss it in handfuls and whisper my name and say how we would be happy for ever.

For ever.

I believed him.

For ever.

I spoke the words over and over inside my head as Teresa brushed with long strokes.

For ever.

Soft strokes; her hand beneath my hair protecting the back of my neck from the prickling of the brush.

I then went downstairs to the drawing room, intending to finish my work on the song.

For my Son

I wrote the words with care in the centre of the page, above the staves.

Then I saw the little bundle of envelopes that I had left on the piano last evening. I have never been able to understand why Patrick always insisted on keeping to himself all records of the boys' progress at school. Maybe it was to do with the fact that I had never wanted them to go away to England to school: I had always been worried that they might become estranged from their own country as well as from their siblings.

'You look after the girls, my dearest Louisa, and leave me to be responsible for the boys. After all, I know how things should be. You are too soft sometimes and have flighty notions in your head.'

That, of course, was a reference to my nipped-in-the-bud leanings towards women's suffrage, all those years ago.

The school reports and notes from various masters seemed fair and well thought-out. Arthur was and has always been a dogged and ambitious worker, not brilliant but thoughtful and consistent. Those were the words they used in their cramped writing. 'Reliable and pleasant', his housemaster wrote on one page; 'a boy capable of gaining the confidence of his peers', wrote the head on another; 'he will make an admirable prefect'.

Harry, on the other hand, was less consistent: sports and music were his strong subjects; the sports masters wrote glowing praise of his skill and energy. I remembered as I read how I used to go down to the sea's edge at Paradise to watch him diving like a sea bird cutting into the water then rising again away out in the bay to wave to me. Those were most beautiful moments. He didn't seem to care too much about his book work, sometimes turning in scrappy unconsidered work and occasionally outshining unexpectedly, the best in his class; this irritated his masters. They were unable to pin him down with their comments. He was as elusive to them as a sea bird. I don't think schoolmasters like that very much.

There were none of Gerald's reports among the envelopes, maybe because he didn't go to Rugby. Patrick never told me why.

I held the last envelope in my hand for a few moments before opening it. Written on the back of the envelope in black ink were the words 'Strictly Private'. No one ever has to know, I thought, and then I opened it.

I read it standing by the piano and then I went and sat in the armchair by the window and read it again. The window must have been open as the pages fluttered from time to time in my hands, or else it was my hands that trembled. Yes, that is more like.

The headmaster was insisting that Patrick come and remove Harry from the school for performing frequently gross, shameful homosexual acts. 'The acts are shameful,' he wrote, 'but I fear the boy is shameless. I cannot in all conscience allow this boy to remain in the school. Homosexuality is a sickness that must be stamped out and I hope for the boy's own sake that you will make every effort to cure him or to restrain him in some way from engaging in such acts in the future. His life may be ruined and also the lives of those with whom he comes in close contact.'

A gust of wind made the window rattle in its tall frame. I could not move from the chair, my eyes burned with the heat of dry tears.

I have looked at the Gorgon's head and I have turned to stone. I thought nothing, saw nothing, heard nothing. I couldn't even feel my heart beating.

Teresa came into the room, a long time later; the sun was now making black shadows down the street. She said no word. She crossed the room and rattled the coal bucket and the tongs and shovel. She heaped coal on the evening fire. Then for a moment she stood and looked at me. 'Is everything all right, ma'am?'

With difficulty I turned my head and smiled at her. 'Thank you, Teresa. Everything is as it has always been.'

'The fire will blaze up in a minute or two, ma'am.'

'Yes,' I said. 'The fire.'

'Can I help you over to the sofa, and get the little rug for your knees?'

'No, thank you, Teresa. I will just sit here awhile.'

She left the room, closing the door gently behind her.

I sat on for a while the letter between my fingers.

I understood now, after all these years, why Patrick had sent our seventeen-year-old son to the war.

Our child.

I remember the blue day, blustery August, sun and jaunty clouds, below the bay flicking with white and silver, birds and little waves. Patrick impatient to go, twitching the reins on the pony's back, while the children cavorted and cheered and hugged Harry and joked and clapped as he got into the trap and closed the door with a click like a gunshot. I stood on the steps and couldn't even smile. Harry was pale. He raised a hand towards me. 'Cheer up, Mother. This will all be over soon and I'll be back. Come, wish me well.'

What could I do? I nodded and smiled and waved as they trotted off down the drive, the little ones running after them. Only Millie stood beside me. She touched my arm. 'What will happen to Ireland now, with all the young men gone away?'

How could I answer such a question?

Patrick came back two days later. I was standing in the hall when he came in the door.

'Why?'

He kissed my cheek. 'It will make a man of him.'

It is the sense of failure that overwhelms me, and grief.

Grief for my failure to know my son and by knowing him save him from death. Love is not enough.

Grief for my weakness in not challenging Patrick down the years, in not trusting him to allow himself to be challenged. Love is not enough.

Grief that I have now lost God and will go into the darkness without the conviction that I will see his face.

Grief because maybe I am mad and what a waste of a short life it is to be mad for so long.

I cannot see Patrick again.

Though I would say nothing of what I have read I know that my eyes would be filled with blame.

We must not blame each other. We must try to comfort each other. I have no comfort left.

I will finish my song.

The song for my Son.

Then I will open the windows and play the introduction and sing as best I can Francis Ledwidge's sad words . . . 'sorrow and silence are the wood's threnody, the silence for you and the sorrow for me'.

And the sound will drift out and be swept away along the street with the dust and the rest of the day's debris. After that ceremony is finished I will heap the fireplace with the school reports and the headmaster's letter and the music manuscript book and I will watch until they are burnt. When there is total darkness and the streets are empty I will put on my hat and coat and, very quietly, let myself out of the house. It is uphill to Leeson Street and I will walk as fast as I can past the tall houses, where we used to dance and dine and lead careless lives, past the railed gardens, where the children used to play in the afternoons. I will not loiter, but push my way through the memories to the

*lock gates at Leeson Street bridge. I do hope there will
be a bright moon shining as I would like to be able to
see the distant hills just before the end.*

That is my plan for the rest of my life.

* * *

I cried for her when I read those pages.

I wondered why she had not burnt all these folded
pieces of paper with the music and the letter from the
headmaster.

I presume she wanted Patrick to read them.

I wonder if he did.

Probably not.

They were thrown so casually into the trunk, like
rubbish into a dustbin.

I offer them to Johnny.

It is all that I can do.

* * *

It was a horrible time, those first few months of 1970. Not
only was the weather unpleasant, but we all seemed to be
behaving in some inexplicable way, quite unlike our normal
selves.

Johnny had become impossible, his visits to the house

infrequent and mostly silent, his voice curt, his face unfriendly. He looked wretched and his hands shook from time to time so badly that he had to shove them into his coat pockets so that no one would notice. I presumed that he was working too hard and spending his nights out drinking with his friends.

I knew that Mathilde would scold him if she saw the state he was in, but she didn't get the chance: she had retreated more and more into the basement during those post-Christmas weeks, and if Johnny came to the house he always brought Bruno with him.

Each week we would go to the cinema, he and Bruno and I. He would say little and always determinedly sit between Bruno and myself in the cinema, so that I was unable to have the comfort of Bruno's hand on my knee or his arm around my shoulders. I resented this and sulked, so the weekly outings became more a torment than a treat. Bruno would catch my hand and kiss it when he thought Johnny wasn't looking or touch the side of my face with a finger as he helped me off with my coat or wrapped my scarf carefully around my neck. I continued with the outings in the hope of such tiny moments of joy.

I was distracted by my love for Bruno, and was pained and angered by the fact that I never saw him alone any more. I was convinced that each touch or glance meant that my feelings were reciprocated and I couldn't understand why he didn't make more effort to see me. I blamed Johnny's moodiness for Bruno's lack of attention. I found it hard to concentrate on my schoolwork and I was constantly in trouble for my sloth and carelessness. I was truly obsessed by thoughts of him. Sometimes I would think I smelt his aftershave on the landing outside my bedroom and my heart would begin to thud. Once I was woken in the early hours by what I thought to be a little spurt of his laughter and from time to time I heard his footsteps running lightly down the stairs. Coming home from a friend's house after dark one evening, I saw a figure that I thought to be his move through the lamplight near our gate. I called out his name and ran to meet him, but no one answered, no one moved, no one was there.

I hated such hauntings.

One day after school I let myself in at the hall door and was immediately aware of the spicy scent he always wore. I ran into the drawing room. Sylvia was alone, sitting on the sofa reading the paper. She looked up and smiled at me. 'Hello, Imogen. How wet you are. How utterly soaking wet. Run along and change at once or you'll catch a chill. If you go down to Mathilde she'll give you a cup of tea.'

'Is Bruno here?'

She looked surprised. 'Bruno? Were you expecting him?'

'No. I . . . just . . . I thought I . . .'

'Run along and change.'

I felt absurd. I felt more than that: I felt a little crazy.

I went and took off my shoes and hung my wet coat and scarf in the cloakroom, then returned to the drawing room. It was empty and the 'Irish Times' lay neatly folded on the sofa.

I went down into the basement.

The radio was playing softly and Mathilde was sitting by the fire, knitting. She knitted jerseys and skirts and little round multicoloured caps that she used to send off in neat packages to various addresses in Eastern Europe. I always wondered if they arrived safely, but she never seemed to have such doubts. She was working on some very convoluted floral pattern that required her full attention in weaving the wools backwards and forwards, on and off the needles. She didn't look up when I came in.

'Flute and harp. Mozart,' she said. She always liked to tell me what was playing. She loved Mozart. 'My little sweetheart,' she used to call him. 'We have walked down the same streets, he and I.'

'Not at the same time,' I said to her once, being clever.

'So, what does that matter? If I were to go back there now, this moment I could hear his footsteps if I stood to listen.'

Anyway, she said, 'Flute and harp. Mozart,' as I came in at the door.

I said nothing.

Carefully she finished her line of knitting, then stuck the needles into the wool and put the garment away in her work-basket.

'What do you think is the matter with everyone?'

'Is bad February. February is always bad. There is too much darkness. It whispers into people's heads.'

'What does?'

'The darkness.'

That seemed reasonable to me. Maybe when March came and the light and things began to shake themselves, everything would get better.

'In Norway, in Finland, they kill themselves in the winter. Have you homework to do?'

'A bit.'

'Sit there at the table and I will make some tea. No need to do your homework in loneliness. And out of the sides of your ears you can listen to Mozart.'

Mathilde was always right.

* * *

Letter from my great-grandfather (Patrick) to my grandfather (Arthur) and for some reason never sent.

Thursday evening.

My dear Arthur,

Thank you for all your hard work. I am sorry to
have burdened you with the sad arrangements,
but I really did not feel up to dealing with such
decisions and discussions. I think we have done
the right thing, and the police and the rector have
been most obliging. There is nothing to be gained
by airing the possibility of suicide: too many hearts
would be broken at such a notion. We will keep
our speculations strictly *entre nous*.

I don't think that you should tell Helen, but that
is, of course, up to you.

I have no idea, apart from her debilitated state of
health over the last few years, as to why she should
have done such a thing. She was always so
thoughtful of the feelings of others and she must
have known the pain that such an ending of her life
would cause. I see nothing to be gained by telling
Gerald, and certainly not the girls, though I believe
that Millie suspects the worst. She will be discreet.

It is because she left no message that the police
are prepared to turn a blind eye. I had a very nice
letter from the City Commissioner himself
commiserating on my great loss and the 'tragic
accident' that caused it.

Please thank Helen for her kind invitation to
stay for a while, but I think I must accustom
myself to life here alone. It must go on. Work is
now the impetus and, of course, Millie comes and
goes, one crazy scheme after another in her head.
The servants are staunch, though Teresa weeps too
much. We must all struggle to retain normality as
a family. This is really still the aftermath of that
terrible war.

I remain your affectionate father.

✢ ✢ ✢

I remember so well coming into the house that night.

The hall light was on and the lights on the stairs and the
landing above. There was no sound, no drifting music from
Mathilde's rooms, no footsteps, no voice calling out a
greeting, only the spicy smell of Bruno hanging in the warm
air. I had been round having supper at the house of a friend
and we had had some spat of words and I had left early to
come home. I ran up the stairs and, crossing the landing, I
noticed that Sylvia's bedroom door was open and a light was
shining in her room. I stepped into the doorway to say good
night. Luckily I didn't say a word. I stood in silence and they
never noticed my presence. The smell of him was intensified
by the heat of his burrowing body. That was all I could

think of, burrowing and the smell of spices. It was as if he were trying to beat his way back inside her body, back into her dark womb. My mother's womb.

My mother welcoming his intrusion, straining and pulling him into her, sobbing with the effort to imprison him inside her.

I stepped back out of the room and stood on the landing unable to move, afraid that they might hear a creaking board, a step, a gasp, even a breath. I tried for a moment to stop breathing. I tried to stop my heart beating. I tried to stop existing.

I remember putting my hands over my face, like a child hiding: this made me invisible. I knew that if either of them came to the door at that moment they would not be able to see me. I felt safe with my face covered. I began to breathe again. I realized that I had to get away from that rooted spot. Escape. Run silently.

I moved to the top of the stairs.

I took my hands from my face. They were wet.

I must be crying, I thought.

Bugger, I thought. At this moment I want to die, not flood the world with tears.

The top step creaked softly under my foot.

I paused for a moment, then ran down to the hall. It was safer there. I have to find Johnny, I thought. Only with Johnny will I be really safe.

On the table in the hall was a large silk scarf. I snatched it up and tied it, Queen of England style, round my head. It felt soft and very expensive. I opened the hall door and went out and down the granite steps. A fierce wind was blowing along Lansdowne Road and I ran head down into it, clutching at my coat with both hands as it seemed likely to be torn off me and blown away. After a couple of minutes I decided that running was silly. I must walk, I must control my heart and my lungs and, indeed, my legs, which trembled with each step I took.

Where am I going?

I asked myself that question aloud, and for a moment couldn't answer it. To Johnny. It had to be to Johnny. Johnny would comfort me. He would behave like a grown-up. He would love me and tell me what to do. There was a bus just drawing in to the stop and I ran across the road waving at the driver. He waited for me and I climbed the stairs and sat in the front seat.

I took off the scarf and looked at it: it was heavy crêpe-de-Chine, a deep rosy pink with a tumbling snake-like pattern woven through it in shades of yellow and pale brown, hand-rolled edge, so big that you could have worn it wrapped round you from neck to knee. Too exotic for the Queen of England, I thought. Really, when push came to shove, too exotic also for Sylvia.

Maybe Bruno had found her exotic.

I stared at the scarf, hoping that the snake-like pattern would transform itself into some kind of message.

'What's up?' asked the conductor.

His voice startled me. He was standing beside me, rattling the coins in his satchel.

I shook my head.

'Been having a good old bawl?' he said. 'That's the girl. Get it off your chest, and between you, me and the wall he isn't worth it, love. Where to?'

'Clare Street.' I handed him the money and he rolled a ticket out of his machine.

'We've all been there, love,' he said. 'We all get over it.'

He disappeared down the stairs with a wave.

I looked at my reflection in the dark window. Raindrops chased each other down the outside of the glass. I looked dreadful.

Raindrops and tears mixed on my reflected face. Hot, stupid eyes stared back at me. They had to be stupid eyes.

I picked up the scarf and rubbed at my face with it, then blew my nose into its softness. I laughed for a moment after I had done that, and then I did it again. I blew and blew until my head was dizzy and my nose was clear. I crunched the scarf up and threw it under the seat, where it joined a couple of crisp bags and an apple core; nothing exotic.

When I got off in Clare Street the conductor waved at me again. 'Don't worry, love, it may never happen.'

Perhaps he might find the scarf and bring it home to his wife and she might wash it and wear it and enjoy it, wrap it round herself from neck to knee and laugh with pleasure at how exotic she looked.

I ran through College Park.

The light was on in Johnny's room.

I stood below on the path looking up.

Footsteps rattled on the stairs and the man from Athlone came out of the door. He looked at me for a moment.

'Hi,' he said.

'Hi.'

He turned and looked up at the window. 'Johnno,' he yelled. 'Johnno. Little sister.' He nodded at me and walked off towards Front Square. After a few steps he turned round and gestured with a hand. 'Go on up.'

As I went up the stone stairs I heard the door above me open. Johnny came out on to the landing. 'What the fuck are you doing here, Im?'

'Johnny. I've—'

'Bloody persecuting me. Can I have no life of my own? Every time I move you're there. There, there, there. Everywhere. It's the bloody middle of the bloody night, for heaven's sake.'

I was up beside him and I took his arm and pulled him into his room. 'You're drunk.'

'So? What business is it of yours if I'm drunk? Or if I'm sober or stoned or mad or sane. It's none of your . . .'

I pushed him down into a chair. He fell asleep. His eyes closed and his head rolled forward, his whole body went quite limp and, for a moment, I thought that he was dead. I stood and watched him sleeping for a few minutes and then I went into the kitchen and filled a bowl with cold water. I wasn't sure what to do next, so I stood again and watched him sleep for about ten minutes and then I threw the water into his face. He shook his head and I was reminded of him after a dive, when he would rise up triumphantly out of the sea and shake the shining drops from his head and I would cheer. He opened his eyes and brushed the water from his face with a hand.

His eyes focused on me. 'Im.'

His voice was startled but subdued. He looked at his wet hand, wiped at the water running down his neck. 'What is this? What is . . . Im. What's been going on?'

He struggled to his feet; water dripped on to the floor. He shook his head again. 'Jesus,' he said. 'Jesus fucking Christ.'

I sat down at the table and started to cry.

He touched my shoulder.

'Hang on, sis, just . . . hang . . . just a tick . . . I don't know . . . just a . . .' He left the room and I cried on, my head in my hands. I heard a tap running and in a moment he came back into the room. I looked up at him. He was rubbing at his face and hair with a towel. 'Did you do this to me?'

I nodded.

'I presume you have some reason?'

I didn't answer. I was frightened now. I didn't know what to say. I thought that if I began to speak he might throw me out and then what would I do?

He sat down beside me and took my hand. 'Come on, Im. I'm sorry I yelled at you. I'm just a bit out of my mind, these days. Come on. What's up? Something's up. I can see that. You look awful.'

'So do you.'

We smiled at each other. He pressed my fingers tight. 'Look,' he said, after a long time, 'would this have anything to do with Bruno?'

'Well . . .'

'You were at the pictures with him.'

I shook my head.

'Yes.' He spoke the word sharply. 'He told me he was taking you to the pictures and he didn't want me to come. "Two's company" were the words he used. Here.' He took a surprisingly clean handkerchief from his pocket and handed it to me. 'Blow your nose.'

I obeyed.

'So, what happened?'

'He never asked me to go to the pictures. Never. Only those times we all went together. I found him with Sylvia.' Silly way to put it, I thought.

He looked puzzled. 'You . . . ?'

'Sylvia. Mother.'

'What exactly do you mean?'

'In bed.' I started to cry again. 'Earlier. I came home and . . . Oh, Johnny, I had to . . . I'm sorry I came bursting in on you, but I had to . . . I had to . . .'

He took my other hand in his and pulled me close to him. 'Easy, Im. Just take it very easy and tell me. Start at the beginning. You were out?'

'I was at Siobhan's and I came home about nine, about nine, yes. And I went upstairs and her door was open and I saw them.'

'Saw them?'

'Yes. Don't ask me to give you all the details. I saw them. There. On the bed. With no . . . Naked.'

'Are you sure?'

'What do you mean, am I sure? Amn't I telling you? You think I'm making this up?'

'Are you sure it was Bruno?'

'Of course I'm sure. I saw his face as clear as I see yours

now. I know his face so well I . . . Yes. It was Bruno. And Sylvia. They looked like . . .'

'What?'

'Like they wanted to eat each other alive.'

His face had gone from splotchy red to white. His head drooped on to my shoulder. I could smell the drink from his skin. He made a thin, high screaming noise, like a small animal caught in a trap. I put my arms around him. 'Don't, please, Johnny, don't.'

I was the one who should be crying. He should be comforting me. I held him. I felt his hot tears on my neck. What a wet mess we were in the two of us. 'Ssssh. There.' I stroked his back, his wet hair, his arms, his hands. I hugged him to me and thought how fragile he had become. We needed Mathilde, but this time we would have to get through pain without her.

Johnny was speaking.

'I love him so much . . . Forget what I say. Listen. No, no. Do not listen. So bloody much love. I thought . . . Do not listen. Oh, God, how can I say such things to you? A child? Listen. Do not listen. Forget. Yes, that is it. You must forget. I love him so much. How can he do this . . . And I knew . . . I know he loves me. Yes. Forget. Im. Im. Im. What can I do now? Where can I go? I have to go. What am I? That is what they will say? How . . . ooooh, how can I continue to live without him? Im . . . Im . . . sister, forget.'

I didn't know what the hell he was trying to say. I heard some words and not others. I kept hearing, 'Forget, forget.' I kept hearing, 'Go.' I must go, I kept thinking, and yet I could do nothing, only stroke him. Finally he became quiet and we sat in silence with our arms tight around each other. I thought about his jumbled words; slowly, I realized what he had been saying. I put my hand to his face and turned it towards me. 'Do you mean that . . . ?'

His eyes were so huge and so blue and so damaged by drink and tears that I could hardly bear to look into them.

'That you and he . . . that . . .'

'Yes.'

'That makes it all very complicated.'

'Yes.'

'Have you . . . has he . . . ? I mean, for how long?'

'Since the first moment he came into the school. I just knew. He looked at me and . . . well, I can't explain. I'm sorry, Im.'

'Why sorry? Why didn't you tell me? That's the only thing to be sorry about, that you didn't tell me. Couldn't you see that I was . . . well, sort of potty about him?'

He mumbled something that I couldn't hear. 'What? I can't hear what you're saying.'

'We thought that was quite funny.'

'Funny?'

'I honestly didn't think you'd take it seriously. Honestly.'

I seriously considered hitting him, but thought the better of it. Anyway, what would be gained? Nothing. More tears. More, 'Sorry, Im.' More running out into the rain and finding another bus home. I would have to go home, I realised that, but I was bloody well going to make him pay for a taxi.

'Maybe this is quite funny too.'

'Im!'

'Do you think he'll have told Sylvia about you? Maybe they think that's funny. That queer stuff . . . There's a hell of a lot of funny stuff going on all round the place, ha, ha ha.'

'He wouldn't do that.'

'No?' I got up. 'I'm going home. Why don't you come with me? A hot bath and a comfortable night in your own bed . . .'

'You sound like Mathilde.'

'Yes. Maybe she's right. Such unimportant things do give comfort. Mathilde should know. I think Mathilde has suffered more than you or I ever will. Or Father or Sylvia.'

'I don't want Father to know . . .'

'He won't. He's always somewhere else in his head. He wouldn't mind about you anyway. He's not the sort of person who would mind a thing like that.'

'I don't want him to know about . . . me.'

'No one will know, unless Bruno tells her. No one, Johnny. We can all lie, cheat and dissemble. Keep secrets tight in our head. Maybe one day we'll even forget that we have secrets. Or maybe one day it won't matter any more.'

'What are you going to do?'

'Nothing. Come home with me. I'll feel stronger if you come with me.'

'No. I can't.'

'He won't be there. He'll be gone by now. I think he's been slipping in and out of the house for weeks. Come.' I held out my hand to him.

He shook his head. He took my hand. 'Tell me. Do you mind? Do you think I'm disgraceful?'

'No. You're Johnny. Look, I'm dead. I want to go even if you won't come with me. I can't talk any more tonight. Sometime when you're sober and we're not in shock. Perhaps. But you're Johnny. The other thing doesn't matter. Not at all. Not ever.'

'What will I do?'

'I can't possibly answer that. Recover. I'm going to have to recover. You must do that too. I'd give up the bottle and whatever else you're shoving inside yourself. Clear out your brain.'

'Thanks, Marjorie Proops.'

'Any time. My advice comes free . . . well, not exactly, now I come to think of it. Have you the price of a taxi on you? I need a taxi to get home. I don't want to cry all over a bus conductor again.'

He put his hand into his pocket and pulled out some crumpled notes and shoved them into my hand.

'Thanks.'

'I'll walk with you to the taxi rank.'

'It's OK. I'll be OK. You stay here. You look grim. Go to bed. I'll see you. We'll talk. We'll make things work out.'

I headed for the door. As I opened it he came up to me. 'Im.'

'Yes.'

'You won't say a fucking word, will you?'

'No.' I kissed his cheek. 'No.'

'Promise.'

'Cross my heart and hope to die.'

The house was more alive when I got home. There was a light in Mathilde's sitting room, and as I opened the front door the sound of a counter-tenor came from the drawing room. I stood and listened.

Stabat mater dolorosa.

And then a soaring boy's voice.

Justa crucem lacrimosa,
Dum pendebat filius.

'Imogen.'

I went to the drawing-room door. 'Yes, Father.'

He sat in the semi-darkness, just one light shining down over his shoulder. He looked tired. 'I didn't know if you were in or not. Had a good evening?'

'Yes, thank you.' Lie number one.

Cuius animam gementem,
Constritatum, ac dolentum . . .

'Everything all right?'

Pertransivit gladius.

I nodded.

'I'll lock up, now that I know you're in. Run along to bed. Sleep well. You look exhausted.'

'Good night, Father.'

'Good night, daughter.'

I went slowly up the stairs, the voices of sadness following me and also the voice of Johnny.

Promise.

Cross my heart and hope to die.

The scent of Bruno still lingered on the landing. My mother's bedroom door was shut, no crack of light to be seen.

Promise.

Cross my heart and hope to die.

> *O quam tristis et afflicta*
> *Fuit illa benedicta*
> *Mater unigeniti.*

✲ ✲ ✲

I slept.

Sleep is such a strange thing: sometimes for no reason you toss and turn and twitch and sigh and bang the pillows all night long, and then other times, when your whole world is falling apart, you sleep like a baby the moment your head hits the pillow.

I slept sweetly, no dreams, no startled jerks into wakefulness, no disturbances of any sort, and when I woke in the morning I discovered that I had lost my voice. Of course, I didn't know for some time. Although I had slept I woke quite unrefreshed, my head in a whirl of confusion, my bones aching as if I had flu. It was still dark and I lay and watched the lights go on in the houses across the road and the sky slowly changing from black to grey, and the cars swished through the puddles. A train clicked through the station and I knew I should get up, but I wanted to stay where I was, to cover my head, to be alone in darkness.

The door opened and Sylvia put her head into the room. 'Imogen, it's time you were up.'

I sat up. My body was invaded by fear and I began to shake.

She pushed the door open further and came into the room. 'It's freezing in here. I can't think why you insist on sleeping with the window open at this time of year.' She walked across the room and pushed the window down. 'Pu-uh. It cannot be good for you.' She looked at me. 'Up. You'll be late for school.'

I wanted to tell her that I couldn't go to school that day, to say that I was ill, but no words would come out of my mouth.

'Up,' she said again, and left the room.

I got up and put on my dressing-gown and went into the bathroom. I looked at myself in the glass. I washed my face and teeth and examined the inside of my mouth. I felt my neck glands. I tried to cough. My mouth opened and closed but no sound came out, not even a tiny whisper. My throat wasn't sore, my glands unswollen.

'Hello,' I tried to say. Pretty banal. No sound. I took several deep breaths. I gargled with mouthwash. 'Hello,' I tried again, and then I became alarmed.

I went downstairs to the dining room, where Sylvia and my father were eating their breakfast. Father was hidden behind the 'Irish Times'; Sylvia stared into space, a faint smile on her face. She looked at me when I came in. 'What's the matter? Why aren't you dressed? Really, Imogen . . .'

Father peered from behind the paper. 'Morning. Not going to school?'

I shook my head and pointed to my mouth. 'Sore throat?' asked Sylvia. 'It's going round.'

I shook my head again and taking her hand I held it against my throat.

She felt my glands with her fingers. 'Nothing wrong there. Sit down, dear, and have a cup of tea. That will loosen things up in your throat.' She put her hand on my forehead. 'I don't think she's feverish.'

'Perhaps she should go back to bed,' said my father. 'She looks pretty rotten. Not much point in her going to school if she can't speak.'

'Sit down and have your breakfast, and then you can go back to bed. We'll see how things progress during the day. There's no point in getting the doctor out on a fool's errand.'

I had some breakfast and I went back to bed. I thought about Johnny and my mother and Bruno, and tried from time to time to speak, but no words would come.

Mathilde arrived up with a cup of coffee for me. 'Invalid.' I nodded.

She put the coffee on the table beside my bed. 'Lost your tongue, eh?'

I nodded.

'No harm for a day or two. Give us all a rest.'

I felt the tears sliding down my face.

Mathilde sat down on the bed and put her arms around me. 'It's all right, little Imogen. It's all right. There has been too much going on for your brain to catch hold of. You are only a baby, after all. A young, sad baby.'

Then I knew that she knew. The tears slipped silently down my cheeks and she wiped them and she held my hand. 'So, you lose your tongue? I have known in the past another young girl to lose her tongue. It is not uncommon. Time will heal you. But for these days you must write messages.' She produced out of the pocket of her skirt a notepad and a ballpoint pen. She put them on the table. 'It will be hard for you, if you decide not to write messages. It makes you very vulnerable to their decisions. Think, Imogen, before it is too late.'

My head was tired and hot and lonely. I closed my eyes. I knew she was right. I knew I had to think, but I felt I had no capacity to do so. I opened my eyes. I would at least smile at her so that she would know I had no ill-will towards her, but she was not there. I wondered if she had been there at all. I turned my head and looked at the table. The notepad and the pen were where she had left them. I knew I would not be able to use them. I knew the pen would be too heavy for my hand to hold.

Days floated past.

They came and went and I lay and watched them, Sylvia lively but increasingly anxious, Father bemused, and Dr Lavery, who shook his finger at me and shone his torch down my throat, frowned and spoke to my mother out of the side of his mouth.

I didn't want to get up and wander speechless round the house: I preferred to lie in bed, half asleep, my head filled sometimes with dreams and sometimes with nightmares.

'At least get up,' Sylvia said to me one morning. 'There is nothing wrong with you. Think of poor Mathilde, carrying trays up and down, down and then up again.'

Mathilde had this great facility for coming into the room at just the right moment. She rustled in at that moment with a cup of milky coffee. 'Poor Mathilde!' she said. 'I do not like to be called that. I have my full health and strength. I can walk upstairs and downstairs all day long if I wish, and I do not wish to be called poor Mathilde.'

'She might recover quicker if you didn't spoil her like this. She just needs to pull herself together.'

'I doubt,' said Mathilde, and left the room.

'We think, your father and I, that — and, of course, Dr Lavery, that perhaps you need psychiatric help.'

I opened my mouth hoping for the first time that some sound would come out, some cry of protest, but of course it didn't.

'We think, and we have done a lot of thinking in the last few days, that perhaps you are suffering some kind of nervous breakdown. Why? None of us can answer that. You could, I presume, if you would, maybe not. There are a lot of things that happen in the brain that are inexplicable. Neither your father nor I nor, indeed, Dr Lavery is really competent to diagnose or treat you in the state you are in. So . . .' She paused for a long time. She walked over and looked out of the window.

I wanted to speak. I am not mad, I wanted to say. I am not mad, just weary with events, burdened by discovery.

Perhaps growing up was going to prove to be too much for me. I didn't really think so but I needed time, not psychiatric help. Time here in my own room. I needed the comfort of love.

She was talking. I had not been listening so I caught her grey words mid-sentence.

'. . . in your best interests. We want to get you back on the rails as soon as possible. It's a lovely place, darling. It really is.'

She came over and laid her hand most tenderly on my head. She bent and kissed my forehead. She smoothed my hair. I looked at her, questions in my eyes. She smiled. Her wonderful smile. I hated her.

She seemed to sense this and withdrew her smile and her hand from my head. 'We have arranged to bring you down tomorrow, your father and I, and then we can . . . well, deal with the formalities. I assure you . . . I promise you that you will get the best possible . . . The best . . .'

I turned round and pushed my face into my pillows and covered my ears with my hands.

I remember very little more except Mathilde throwing her arms around me in the hall at the last moment. 'It will be well, child,' she said, and I saw that she was crying.

I clung to her.

My father coughed apologetically and Sylvia took my arm, and we walked slowly out into the rain.

Again I remember my silent tears.

And again.

And again.

* * *

I have little more to say.

I spoke to Mathilde one day, not long before she went into hospital. We were sitting as we always had done in her sitting room by the fire that she always lit, winter or summer; she seemed to need the comfort of it, rather than the warmth. I still enjoy the old-fashioned conversational murmur of a fire and how furniture comes to life in the flickering light.

That evening as we sat there she seemed old to me; I do

have to say that she had never seemed young to me, just an unchanging, secure part of my life. But at that moment by the fire, I felt that she might disappear out of my life and Father's life, and we would feel the loss of her as I certainly had not felt the loss of Mother.

'Mathilde.'

She looked up from her knitting. 'Child?'

'Can you talk to me a bit about Sylvia? I remember so little. Just a shadowy figure, really, like a ghost. I feel bad about that. People should know about their mothers.'

She gathered her knitting together, stuck the needles into the wool and packed everything neatly into her knitting-bag. She took off her glasses and put them on the table. She had taken to wearing glasses a few years before, but never when she was talking. It was as if she felt they separated her from the person to whom she was talking; a whole pane of glass rather than two little round circles.

'If you don't mind,' I said.

'Now is as good a time as any.'

Her eyes were pale grey and veiled as if by early-morning mist, but the firelight sparked in the mist from time to time and made her look young.

'It is very difficult to have nothing, only terrible memories and the huge question mark in your mind, always. Why am I still here? Why me? Why not one of my sisters or my brother? Is it my fault somehow that they are dead?

And all those others? Why me? Should I too not have died? Have I in some way betrayed them all by being still alive?'

She smiled at me.

'Those are not questions for you to worry about. Those are my questions. My private and personal questions. And what I say to you about your mother is that because of her I am still her, still asking the same old questions, though the asking voice in my head is no longer as loud as it used to be. No. Not nearly as loud.'

She leaned forward and touched my knee.

'Your mother . . . and, of course, your father too . . . took me in and gave me a home and, in time, a family. She asked me no questions, she just opened her doors to me. She trusted me, and in the end she gave me Johnny and you to love. Life. That is what I owe her. I thought once upon a time to kill myself, because the questions went on and on shouting in my head and yet here I am, old and yapping like an old cross dog. A cross old woman, but I'm here. All that life I give to your mother. I say thanks. I will always say thanks.' She made a strange little salute with her right hand.

'Thank you,' I said.

'It was that boy, that . . .'

'Bruno.'

'Yes, that Bruno, that Bruno, that Bruno. He just left her when things went wrong. When you . . . He just dumped her like rubbish. And went. Piff. I do not know where he went.

I have never cared where he went. But she and Johnny were going crazy. Crazy for what? I asked myself that so many times. And you, like a little bird shut in a cage. But I knew you would be all right. The others I couldn't say, but you, I knew about you. It is as if you are my child.'

'Did Johnny go away with Bruno?'

She shook her head angrily.

'Johnny's dead. I know you have this thought in your head that he is alive somewhere in the world. But listen to me. He is dead. I tell you, Mathilde knows. That German went scuttering away, back where he came from, alone, and good enough for him. What did I always say to you?'

I laughed.

'I remember. You really should get rid of all those old prejudices.'

'I can hate who I like. I can go into my blackness still hating and loving. It's no one's business but mine. Come. I have a bottle of brandy in the cupboard. Up you get like a good girl and fetch it and some glasses and we'll celebrate.'

I did.

We sat across the fire from each other and raised our glasses.

'To a long life, Mathilde. You're not going into any blackness yet.'

'I have had my long life. I have lived through a lot of war, back there. Terrible war, my personal war. Yes. There.

And then here, in this country. I have felt at times that I shouldn't have come here, that I brought the war trailing with me. I now want peace.'

'The peace that passeth all understanding?'

'That will suit me very nicely.'

* * *

Dear Johnny,

I address this directly to you, wherever you may be, whoever you have chosen to be.

I wonder what name you have chosen for yourself?

I wonder where you live?

By the sea I feel sure, so that you can swim, dive, roll like a bird through the air and into the waves; come up shining, one hand waving gaily to someone.

Who?

What people are in your life? Friends? Lovers? Enemies? We all have enemies for one reason or another.

What language do you speak to the world?

What history do you tell your friends?

Am I ever in your dreams?

Such a load of questions and more and more.

For days I could question you. Maybe you couldn't stomach that thought. I suppose I couldn't blame you for it.

I have to say that I have passed the years without too much pain. I haven't actively sought happiness, which as always seemed to me to be a fairly fruitless pursuit, no matter what our allies the Americans feel to the contrary. It comes from time to time, unannounced, unordered, and is always more than welcome; fragile and at the same time life-enhancing.

Perhaps you might consider coming back here now . . . you notice I have not said home. This can no longer be the place you call home. I am aware of that. A short visit, maybe?

There is no longer any reason why you shouldn't come.

Both our parents are now dead, bluntly put, for which I apologise, but there is no other way to write such words.

Sylvia died years ago, 1983 to be exact, in a motor accident on the Bray Road, being driven at speed by a young man of twenty-three. After Bruno, and after you left, she turned more and more to the company of young men. I saw her seldom, but when I did see her, her smile had become more charming than ever, and her eyes glittered like winter stars. She died instantly in the accident, so at least she was saved the anguish of growing old and probably very lonely.

Father died early this winter, a peaceful death, I do have to say. He just crumbled slowly away, still to the end in Lansdowne Road, looked after by a kind middle-aged man called Gregory, who had moved into the house shortly after Mother's death.

I have sold the house and put aside your share for you to do what you like with. I gave Gregory twenty thousand pounds from the price of the sale. I presumed that you would be happy about this. He made the old man's last years so contented. Even Mathilde would have approved.

I want you to come back, purely for selfish reasons, not just to prove to anyone who might be interested that I was right; a weakness of mine, that desire to be right, but also there is always the possibility that we two old acquaintances might become friends. Pass time together.

I will understand if you have no wish to reappear; I will merely regret your decision. I just wish to open a door that has been closed for so many years. I have a picture of you in my mind like an old snapshot, vitality dimmed by time but

still with the smirk of superiority on your face that
I hated so much, but would love to see again. I
would love to think that there was someone in the
world with whom I could share the past and try to
untangle the threads of our inheritance, our
weaknesses and whatever strengths we may have.

It is our past, Johnny.

Great-uncle Harry looks so like you in his
uniform, with his hat tucked neatly under his arm
and his hair flopping on his forehead, against
military rules I am certain. He was so young when
he died. Have you, his echo, lived his life for him?

It was brave, Johnny, if a little cruel, but
undoubtedly brave to swim away into a new life.
He never got the chance to do that.

And our great-grandmother, you should also
become acquainted with her. You should see the
pictures I have of them in my room and read their
fading writing before it is too late. I have, for years
now, taken piano lessons so that I can play the piano
that gave her and our father so much pleasure.

We could make a trip if you liked down to
Paradise, now called Bealtaine.

Do you remember that echo?

There is always the possibility that houses will
have been built all over that side of the bay and

that the echo will have been chased away. We can stand on the jetty and call out and listen for the voices flying back towards us and we can laugh at our absurdities. Or maybe there will be only silence. How very absurd people have become when they can murder echoes.

If you do decide to come, take a taxi from the airport and remember to tell the driver to switch on the meter. My house is easy to find: it is a bright, cheerful yellow, the third gate from the bottom, and in the summer the front garden is filled with roses. Here is a present for you. Whether you come or not, I feel I would like to give you a present. It is such a pity that neither of us will ever hear the music she wrote, but I hope you enjoy the poem just the same.

> *He will not come, and still I wait.*
> *He whistles at another gate*
> *Where angels listen. Ah, I know*
> *He will not come, yet if I go*
> *How shall I know he did not pass*
> *Barefooted in the flowery grass.*
>
> *The moon leans on one silver horn*
> *Above the silhouettes of morn,*

And from their nest-sills finches whistle
Or stooping pluck the downy thistle
How is the morn so gay and fair
Without his whistling in its air?

The world is calling, I must go.
How shall I know he did not pass
Barefooted in the shining grass?

* * *

This is not a novel.

If it were, I might now be able to write about an anxious but, I am certain, joyous reunion.

A knock on the door of a yellow house. I do not have a bell to ring. There wasn't one here when I bought the house and I could never be bothered to have one put in.

Two ageing people stand face to face.

How do you recognize someone you haven't seen for the best part of thirty years?

In my mirror I seem to look the same as I ever did, but in reality I am no longer the distracted child he last saw, but a confident, successful woman, filled still with curiosity and not yet a touch of grey in my hair. I will be standing in the doorway of my yellow house so Johnny will be able to make a pretty good guess at my identity.

But who will I see before me?

What will time and circumstances have done to my brother?

Will I recognize his long nose?

Will he still carry on his lips that rather superior smile?

Will his hair flop on his forehead as it used to do?

Will I feel confident enough to hold out two hands, clasp shoulders, feel the bones under my fingers and kiss the cheeks of this stranger?

Will it be my fate to be the god of happy endings?

THE END

In memory of Francis Ledwidge
killed in France 31 July 1917